Victims of Gravity

~~Davy James-French~~

Victims of Gravity

Colin

from a vocally relaxed

Davy James-French

Banff
1994

The Porcupine's Quill, Inc.

CANADIAN CATALOGUING IN PUBLICATION DATA

James-French, Dayv.
  Victims of gravity

ISBN 0-88984-109-8

I. Title.

PS8569.A95V52 1990   C813'.54   C90-094152-9
PR9199.3.D394V52 1990

Published by The Porcupine's Quill, Inc., 68 Main Street, Erin, Ontario NOB ITO with financial assistance from the Canada Council and the Ontario Arts Council.

Distributed by The University of Toronto Press, 5201 Dufferin Street, Downsview, Ontario M3H 5T8.

In same or different form, these stories were previously published in *The Antioch Review, Canadian Fiction Magazine, Epoch, Grain* and *Prism International*. 'Domestic Order', 'Signals' and 'Victims of Gravity' appeared in *Coming Attractions 4* (Oberon). 'The Day J. Edgar Hoover Died' appeared in *The Macmillan Anthology 3*.

Readied for the press by John Metcalf. The cover is after a serigraph entitled 'Cat and Artist', © Alex Colville 1990 / VIS*ART Copyright Inc. Photo courtesy David Burnett Art Associates Limited.

Printed and bound by The Porcupine's Quill, Inc.
The stock is Zephyr laid, and the type, Ehrhardt.

Contents

'What else can I tell you?'

from *Letters to a Young Poet*, Rilke

＊

These stories are for David Bernhardt.

Ground Cover

THERE'S AN ART to this: the cupped hands should have the fingers spread just enough for the water to flow through, but not space wide enough for the fish to escape. Bob's getting good at it, in his second summer of cleaning the small pool in Mrs. Porter's backyard.

'Gotcha,' he says, and flips another minnow into the pail balanced on the cement edge. The pail is filled with water from the pond and, after capturing the seventeen fish, he uses a second pail to bail out the remaining water, carrying it to the roots of the hedge at the end of the yard. Barefoot, with his jeans rolled up, he squats in the pool to wire-brush the rough concrete. Slimy green pods grip the surface, growing from one week to the next. He refills the pond with the garden hose. He'll let the pail of minnows sit in the fresh water until the temperatures are more or less the same, about the time it takes to mow the lawn. Then he'll empty the pail, with fish, into the pond. So, for all his effort, the water is never completely clean or fresh, not when it's populated.

None of this would be necessary if Mrs. Porter had shelled out for the pump. Two rubber tubes run under the lawn, from the fishpond into the basement of the house, expressly for the purpose of keeping the water circulating, aerated. But Mrs. Porter paid cash for the new house – her husband's insurance, or most of it – two years ago in a seller's market, and insisted the pump was a luxury she couldn't afford. She's living now, according to Bob's parents, on a widow's pension. Bob doesn't know how much this could be but, by his reckoning, she puts away at least a quart of gin and about a carton of cigarettes in the time it takes him to do the lawn and pool. She does, however, seem to know a whole lot of people constantly arriving from Europe, bearing gifts of duty-free Beefeaters and Rothmans.

Although Bob is sixteen months shy of the legal drinking age, Mrs. Porter always has a tall gin-and-tonic prepared for him, placed carefully on a paper napkin in the centre of one of the redwood tables on her patio. Her own drink is dangerously close to the edge of a larger table, which holds the bottles of gin and tonic water, an ice bucket. And there's a large ashtray with a crude, souvenir look, like something impulsively, or desperately, purchased at a craft outlet too close to the Hilton in a resort area. The Markham house contains a few similar items. The late Mr. Porter and Bob's father used to attend conventions together, there's that connection.

Mrs. Porter, in pink terry shorts and a blouse of eyelet lace, moves her chaise periodically, impatiently, to keep out of direct sunlight. She's very pale. 'I have always had a delicate skin,' she says. 'Redheads do, you know.' Only the soles of her feet, facing Bob, are a dusty brown. And, candidly, her hair is red only to about a half-inch from her scalp.

She has a way of lifting her glass to her lips and snapping her wrist to propel the liquid out of the glass and into her mouth that Bob covertly admires. He's afraid to try it now, in case he misses his mouth, or chips a front tooth, but he thinks he might practice on his own, later.

Behind her back, Bob calls her the Widow Porter, with some fondness. The taking care of her, or her property, makes him feel commanding and self-confident. At home, his little sister has hit the age of adolescent obsession, naturally focused on Bob's development. Marcia gets to say, 'I hope you're still grow-ing, you're really not very tall for man' or 'Is that dirt on your face, or did you forget to shave this month?' Her own concerns, however, her periods, girl-friends, her hair, (imaginary) boy-friends, her complexion and weight, warrant a gentle handling to rival the Manhattan Project.

Bob hates sinking to her level, being mature for his age, but sometimes baiting her is too gratifying to resist.

'Marcia,' he says at dinner, *sotto voce*. 'While you were at the mall, someone snuck into your room and touched your pillow.'

'What's this? What's going on now?' their father asks,

responding to Marcia's outraged howling. 'What's upset your sister?'

'Hormones, probably,' Bob says. 'Could you take her away and have her sedated? I'm trying to eat.' He turns to his mother. 'This is a delicious meal.'

'I chop the onions very fine,' she says. 'Then sauté them in butter. Marcia, if you're not going to behave at table, you might like to go to your room.'

'My room,' Marcia shrieks. 'It'll have to be *fumigated.*'

Bob picks up his glass, snaps his wrist. The milk fills his mouth.

MRS. PORTER'S DAUGHTER, Alice, goes to the same high school as Bob. At least she does now, for her senior year. She used to go to the Catholic school, a grey stone building almost in the centre of town, with no front campus, only a circular drive around a larger-than-life Virgin, and an eight-foot-high hedge enclosing the grounds at the back. This school spawned the usual stories, medieval and updated, with as much or as little truth as these stories usually contain: nuns armed with whips, hysterically sensitive to disobedience; walled-up infants sired by priests; purses searched for tampons instead of acceptable napkins; library books of art treasures with 'suggestive' pages razored out; science courses taught without reference to empirical data; nail-studded underwear under the grey tunics; lunchtime mashed potatoes laced with saltpetre.

Alice and Bob nod when they pass in the hall of the public school now, but rarely speak. She hangs out with a group of girls, women, who are, paramountly, well-groomed, like the woman who went to college, but Speedwriting got her her job. They wear skirts and blouses, or dresses, never slacks or jeans. And their shoes are open-toed creations of straps and heels whose function, evidently, is to cause embarrassment by breaking at awkward moments. That, and the creation of a stiff-kneed, straight-backed walk, strained as the induced facial expression.

These shoes make Bob crazy; they're advertisements for willing victims.

They date college men, Alice and her friends, guys who are out of town during the school year.

Bob had the cords of Christmas lights spread over the carpeted floor of Mrs. Porter's living room. These were for the exterior of the house; the tree trimming being a family tradition for the Porters to celebrate alone or, this year, with Alice's boyfriend, Clay, and a family named Wurtle, to arrive from Germany.

Alice and Clay, who was home for the holidays and looking both shorter and heavier than Bob remembered, were downstairs in the television room. Mrs. Porter sat in a wing-back chair at a right angle to the fireplace, talking to Bob while he tried, independently, each of the little light bulbs, until he had two working strings complete.

'Ted used to do that so beautifully, planning in advance just how the colours would end up on the tree. He'd see the whole thing in his head.' Mrs. Porter lit a cigarette. 'He'd say, Dorothy, what would it mean to the real spirit of Christmas if it's not done right? Well, I could only agree. He cared about details, small things others might not consider important.'

Bob tensed. There was a Christmas when the Porters were at the Markhams' for a party. Bob had been pleasantly half asleep, his door slightly ajar, listening to the adult noises from downstairs, the sound of footsteps on the stairs. The hall light was out, but the bathroom door was open and lit the top of the stairs. Even now, diffuse light spilling from a room one removed from his bedroom reminds Bob of Christmas; as does, oddly, the actress Audrey Hepburn.

But that night, there was shuffling, and a coarse whispering, then Marcia suddenly screamed. Everything was explained away in the morning; Ted had too much to drink and confused the doors at the top of the stairs. He'd entered Marcia's dimly-lit room, braced himself against the wall, unzipped his trousers.

Bob's heard, relating to something else, that marriage changes a man. He's willing to concede that death does the same, or changes the perceived man, his life remembered. Still, hearing of the re-created Mr. Porter makes him nervous, like he's standing on a shifting surface, a plane of incomplete understanding.

He unplugged the working lights, started to loop the cord in a careful circle, keeping the glass bulbs from knocking together.

'I'll give it my best shot,' he said. 'The extension cord and ladder are still in the garage?'

'Unless someone's taken them away.' Mrs. Porter went into the kitchen. Bob heard her refill her glass before calling down the stairs. 'Clay, do you want to give Bob a hand? He's ready to put up the lights.'

'No, he doesn't,' Alice called back. 'Jeez, he's only been here for five minutes and I haven't seen him since Thanksgiving.' The volume of the television was raised after this sentence, not loudly enough to cover the two voices.

'I'm afraid Clay can't help you,' Mrs. Porter said as she came back into the living room. 'Poor Alice. It's not just that he's out of town at college, but she's had to make all new friends at school. And she's so used to being popular.'

'That's okay.' Bob bent to pull on his boots. 'I imagine changing schools is pretty rough. Why'd she want to?'

'Listen, if she hasn't learned her morals by now, there's no sense in my paying private tuition.' Mrs. Porter had a fine line of perspiration at the top of her forehead, just below the hairline.

'I guess not,' Bob agreed. He pushed his gloves into the pockets of his jacket; he'd need direct touch to string the lights, to manipulate the clips over the lip of the eavestroughing. 'I'll ring the bell when the lights are done, okay? Then you can let me know if you want anything changed.'

'Just make them nice,' Mrs. Porter said. 'That's all I want. Nice.'

'ASYMMETRICAL,' Marcia explains. 'Everyone is getting them.'

'Do you know what that means?' Mr. Markham asks. 'Asymmetrical?'

'It's like a big wave on this side.' Marcia's hands move around her face, illustrating the haircut she wants. It's late enough in the spring for the dining room to be naturally lit, sunny even at this hour. 'Then this side is cut into like these little spikes.'

'I meant the word.'

'Unbalanced,' Bob says. 'That's what she wants.'

'I don't know why I have to beg for every little thing I want around here.' Marcia's voice starts to rise. 'You people would probably rather I'd just stay home and ossify.'

'It sounds a little old for you,' Mrs. Markham says. 'I'm not sure it's really appropriate.'

'She's right, though,' Bob offers. 'Lots of girls at school have them, even freshmen. It's just a fashion.'

'Well, then, we'll see,' Mrs. Markham says, in the tone that means yes-but-a-little-later.

'Thanks,' Marcia says, after dinner. She's scraping the plates and handing them to Bob to load into the dishwasher. 'For sticking up for me.'

'It's your hair,' he says. 'And it's a renewable resource.'

'What's that? You know, sometimes you can be okay, but mostly I wonder what the point of you is.'

'You do?' Bob looks over at her. 'So do I, some days. But you should wonder for yourself. What's the point of you.' He looks back into the opened dishwasher. 'You'll notice I'm loading this symmetrically.'

'I could get streaks too.' Marcia holds up a glass dish like a mirror.

'Don't push it. Haircut first. Besides,' he adds, 'if it makes you look like a dink, you'll have the summer for it to grow out.'

'ALICE'S MARKS this year will probably win her an IODE scholarship, her counsellor said,' Mrs. Porter announces. It's the second last weekend in May, Bob's third Sunday afternoon of lawn work.

'That's impressive,' Bob says. He sips some of his gin. His ears feel warm. 'So, will she go to the same college as Clay?'

'I'm not sure.' Mrs. Porter swings her legs over the edge of the chaise, to sit up sideways, facing him. She plants her feet flat on the patio stones, and holds her drink between her spread legs. Below her knees tiny black dots speckle the white skin like pencil marks, where the hair is pushing up from the last shaving. 'The two of them, away from home? I really don't know what to think, not these days. Perhaps I should talk to the monsignor. He was a great friend of Ted's, and he's always taken a special interest in Alice.'

'I'm sure he'd be proud.' Bob is deliberately vague with the pronoun. 'About the scholarship.' The hair on his own legs is almost invisible, although it will brighten against his tanned skin, later in the summer.

'Oh, Ted would have expected it, really. He taught that girl she could do anything.' She makes a noise, like a cough, then takes a deep swallow of her drink. 'And now it's only me, with all this to face on my own.' Her eyes shine.

'Mrs. Porter.' Bob gets up from his chair. He raises one hand to put on her shoulder, moves it back and forth in the air, unable to complete the touch. 'Mrs. Porter,' he repeats.

'Oh, never mind,' she says. 'Don't sit here and watch an old woman feel sorry for herself. Run along and do whatever it is you boys do with your free time.'

'Yes,' Bob says. 'I'll come by later in the week.'

'Could you take the hose?' she asks. 'I seem to have run over a rake in the garage and punctured it. The hose, I mean. With the rake. It needs to be patched or replaced or something. It's just one damn thing after another. The story of my life.'

'I'll get it done.'

THE GARDEN HOSE is textured and coloured to resemble a garter snake. Bob has it coiled and hanging from one shoulder as he follows the sidewalk in the direction of home. On Ash Street, a man appears at the top of a driveway, between the garage and the house, and calls down, 'You! Can I talk to you for a minute?'

Bob looks up and down the street. He manages not to point at himself and ask, with raised eyebrows, 'Me?' It always looks stupid, like having to ostentatiously check your wristwatch, or smack your forehead, before turning back the way you were coming from in public; miming an excuse for an invisible audience, explaining the journey's interruption.

The man, wearing cut-off jeans and a madras shirt, starts down the drive. He's thirty or thirty-five, about the same age as most of Bob's teachers. He might be confusing Bob with someone from school, misled by the crest on the printed track shorts and T-shirt Bob's wearing.

'I didn't know how to get a hold of you. I'm glad I caught you,' the man says. Bob has started up the drive, and they meet a little nearer than half-way. 'It's back here.'

The two of them walk through the breezeway to the back yard. The man has decking, oblique lines of pressure-treated wood, taking up easily a quarter of the property. Two men and three women are arranged on and around plastic patio furniture, the newest kind, upholstered without straps of webbing, really good enough to be put in a dining room. They might be a group out of a commercial for diet cola, is what Bob thinks. One of the women is wearing what looks like two lace tablecloths stitched together. She looks up at Bob, makes a low whistle and says, 'My *god.*'

Bob shifts his weight to his other hip and squints into the distance, past the fence at the end of the yard. Two lots away, at an angle, he can see Mrs. Porter's lawn, and Mrs. Porter sitting alone, in the same attitude as when he left. He keeps her hedge clipped low: the streets arc to a common point.

'Rein your ponies, Susan,' the man says. He turns to Bob. 'I'm sorry, my name's Ken. Dave, Claire, Nancy, Alex,' he indicates the others. 'This is the man I've been watching do the lawn work though the back lot.'

'Bob,' Bob says. 'Lawn work?'

'See, there's really not enough grass to justify the mowing, with the decking? Do you think I should just board the whole thing over, or what are my alternatives?'

'Well, you've got options,' Bob says. He slides the hose from his shoulder, puts it on the ground at his feet. 'Someone might put in some kind of bush for ground cover, and kill the grass underneath.'

'Someone might do that, you said. I like that, a careful man,' Ken says. 'I take it you wouldn't?'

'I think you want something, uh, *vertical,* especially with the fence so close.'

'Like something Japanese?' Susan asks.

'Well, yes.' Bob smiles at her. 'Sure. Something Japanese.'

'He's an artist,' Susan says.

'Could you do it?' Ken asks. 'This late in the spring?'

'Me? Oh, I don't *do* this,' Bob says. 'Well, for a friend, but I've got my exams coming up.'

'You don't?' Ken says. 'And I asked you to come up and work for me. Is my face red?'

'You're in high school?' Susan sits up, pulling folds of the tablecloths away from the arm of the chair. *'High school?'*

'And she's off,' the man, Alex, says. 'Susan's peak experience.'

'Susan lived for cool,' Nancy tells Bob, confidingly. 'There are things from which one never recovers.'

'Cool.' Dave rakes his hands through his hair, like he's briskly rubbing a dog. 'She drove me crazy with that word. "That's not cool," she'd say, every time I wanted to do something that wasn't dangerous or illegal.'

'They're jealous,' Susan says, 'because I got to do the Monkey in a cage at the big dance.'

'Monkey in a cage?' Bob repeats. He thinks he must have missed something. Susan stands up, looking very bored, with her bottom lip stuck out in a pout. She snaps her arms up and down in front of her body, lifts her feet independently, like she's climbing stairs or stepping over hot sand at the beach. The tablecloths jerk and shimmy until she sits down again. She swallows the last of her drink and holds out her glass. Claire takes it from her and puts it down on the table, shaking her head.

'It doesn't look right without a lot of white lipstick and black eyeliner,' Susan apologizes.

'Hey,' Bob says. 'It looked cool.'

'Somebody get Bob a drink,' she says. 'I guess you don't have go-go girls any more.'

'I don't think the student council could afford the Go Gos.' Bob takes an opened beer handed to him by Ken. 'Didn't they break up?'

'Jesus,' Claire moans, 'it's a group. 'How did it happen, that we got old? Didn't we take a vow that we wouldn't?'

'Maybe we just got different. I bet high school is pretty much the same now as it was when I was twelve,' Susan says.

'You were in high school when you were twelve?' Bob considers his sister, her grade school behaviour. Marcia would never dance in front of a stranger, not without the safety net of her friends doing the same, all very deliberately being unaware of each other but moving in unison the way plants on the floor of the sea are waved by invisible currents.

'No, but I went out with boys who were. My mother forgot to tell me not to. I thought it was fun, they had cars and lots of money.' She pulls the tablecloths closer around her body. 'But nobody at my own school would talk to me. Except these twins who were very, uh, gregarious.' She looks down at her lap.

Bob uses his thumbnail to start peeling the label from his beer. His attention is focused on this action when Claire says, 'Well, Susan, you were rather promiscuous.'

He looks up quickly, from Claire to Susan. It's Susan who meets his gaze.

'I didn't think anyone would go out with me. I had acne all over my chest. So if I had a date, I couldn't shame myself, taking off my blouse. I'd take off my pants, instead.'

'Things aren't that different,' Bob says. 'I don't know anyone with acne on her chest, but there're the Bradshaw sisters. They're not twins, though.' And, since he's the stranger here, and has nothing else to offer her, he adds, 'The older one has already been given early admission to pre-med. She's going to be a surgeon.'

'Thank you,' Susan says, very quietly. Bob puts his bottle on the ground, picks up the hose and fits it over his shoulder. 'Ken,' he says. 'I can come back, next weekend, if you want to talk about the lawn.'

ON WEDNESDAY AFTERNOON, almost as soon as Bob gets home from school, there's a phone call from Mrs. Porter. 'I should have got back to you,' he says. 'I think the hose is beyond repair.' The phone cord hangs between him and the wall. He puts one arm out, stiff, and does a few isometric push-aways.

'Never mind about that. Or, rather, do, but not yet. I'm calling to invite you for Saturday. Alice and Clay are getting married.'

'I'm —' Bob starts. 'What?'

'Well, I'm just amazed at myself for being able to keep a secret for so long, but I can tell you now that they were engaged at Christmas.' Mrs. Porter speaks very quickly, as if reading something already committed to memory. 'Can you imagine it, my not giving that away? In one of our nice conversations.'

'Well, sure.' Bob takes his hand from the wall, tucks it between his upper arm and body. 'A secret, after all.'

'She would very much like you to come to the wedding. And Clay, of course. I'm planning a small reception, to be held in the yard. It's so pretty, this time of year. Just a few people.'

'I'm glad to be invited.' Bob is guessing at a correct response. 'What time is the service?'

'Three, at St. Anthony's. Up past the corner? I thought maybe you'd be able to come over early, if you could, and sort of get the lawn into the best possible shape. I'm thinking of paper covers for the tables, very plain, and mostly finger foods.' There's a series of clicks, as though she were tapping a pencil or pen against the receiver or her teeth. 'If you were here about nine, it'd give you lots of time to go home and change, before.'

'I see, yes,' Bob says. There's a silence through the line, which he tries to ride out, but he ends it by adding, 'I guess now what we do is hope for good weather.'

'You do that,' Mrs. Porter says. 'You pray for that.'

'I THINK nothing too personal,' Mrs. Markham says.

'Or expensive,' her husband interjects.

'Who,' she asks, shaking her head slightly, 'made comments about a certain uncle's ignorance of the difference between sterling and plate?'

'After twenty-six years, she remembers,' Mr. Markham mutters, but he's smiling. 'A young man wanting the best for his bride.'

'An appliance or something?' Bob asks. It's his first wedding.

'I don't think so. Those are easier for the family to give, they can compare notes. Maybe glasses. Not crystal, everyday.'

'Well,' Marcia says. 'Why don't you get her something she really needs?'

'Like what?'

'A gift certificate for Abortion City. You rape, we scrape. No fetus can beat us,' she squeals, managing to push her chair back from the table and be out of the room before Mr. Markham can rise from his own place. She calls down, from the safety of the stairs, 'It's like living with the Waltons. Am I only one in the family who isn't a *retard* or something?'

'Where does she hear things like that?' Mr. Markham asks the ceiling.

'Public television,' Bob says. 'But if she's eating off the same plates as the rest of us, we'd better get a dishwasher with a Sani-Cycle.'

'BRIDE OR GROOM?' the man asks. Bob recognizes him as a friend of Clay's from high school two years earlier, although only his face is familiar. He's wearing a blue blazer and slacks, both shiny, although they have no other evidence of long wear.

'What? I was invited,' Bob says. When the question is explained to him, which side of the church he's to be seated on, he apologizes, 'Sorry, I've never been to a wedding before.'

'Listen,' the man says, leaning close. 'You take precautions on your own, know what I mean, and maybe you won't be sorry going to another one.'

'Sure.' Bob slides into the pew, one row behind the empty first. When Mrs. Porter walks down the aisle, with another couple, she looks through him, distracted. Her sleeveless dress is white linen and she's wearing a wide-brimmed hat almost the same colour as her hair. When he arrived at her house, earlier, she and Alice were both in bathrobes, each moving through the house in eccentric patterns with no purpose understandable to Bob, like those wind-up cars that bump into walls, reverse, turn, bump again. Mrs. Porter had stopped long enough to accept the wrapped package Bob offered Alice; a Corningware casserole he'd bought at the same hardware store as the replacement hose.

'That's very thoughtful,' she said. 'Practical.'

'Terrific,' Alice said. 'Our pattern and colour and everything.' She had cellotape over her bangs and spoke without using many of the muscles in her face.

'Alice,' Mrs. Porter said, and Bob understood the tone, but not the warning. They followed him to the basement and stood by the stationary tubs while he fitted the new hose.

'See my ring?' She held out her hand. There was a thin gold wire, a small diamond. 'Here,' she tugged it from her finger. 'You can try it on.'

Bob slipped the ring onto his pinky, as far as it would go between the first and second knuckles, and turned his hand up to look. The diamond flashed like the minnows when, for a brief time, he had them trapped in the shallow basin of his cupped palms. The gold band was hot against his skin. He returned the ring to her, sliding it onto the finger she extended.

'It must have been hard for you, not to wear it at school,' he said. He could imagine the discussions it would provoke at the cafeteria table she shared with her friends during sixth-period lunch; their importantly lowered voices, their quick, sideways glances to surrounding tables, studiously indifferent.

'School?' Alice repeated. 'Oh, since Christmas, you mean. It wasn't easy, not letting anyone know. You can't keep a secret forever.'

'Bob probably wants to get started on the yard,' Mrs. Porter said. 'It's a perfect day, thanks to his prayers.'

Bob looks across the aisle to the groom's side. There are maybe a dozen people in the first three rows. Clay's parents are easy to spot. With a small shock, Bob realizes this is because they alone are not his age, or very near to it. These are boys and girls he's looking at, the other guests, and they're dressed up as adults, as couples from a sit-com about young professionals. He sits on his hands, then moves them out from under his thighs, ready to follow the responses to the service. He doesn't know the ritual, but his impersonation is accurate, only a beat late. At some point, undistinguished from the moments around it, Clay and Alice become husband and wife.

THE YARD looks like a football field after a home-town loss. Plastic cups, paper plates and napkins are strewn across the grass, tossed down when Clay's best man turned up the stereo for dancing. The sun is setting and the lights turned on around the patio define that space with its own yellow aura. The red-wood furniture has been pushed back from the tiles into the encroaching darkness. Bob gets up from his chair and carries his glass into the kitchen to refill his drink. He thinks he must be drunk, considering the amount of gin he's put away, but nobody's giving him any cues if they disapprove.

Alice's Uncle Art is sitting at the kitchen table. He works for a hospital or a union, or a hospital union; Bob doesn't remember which, or if he's Mrs. Porter's brother or brother-in-law. He has a glass pitcher of martinis in front of him, and a tumbler. His wife Vivian is standing in front of the sink. She has a dishtowel neatly tucked into the belt of her dress and an air of knowing exactly what she's doing.

'Get you something, hon?' she asks, shaking a wet ashtray over the sink before placing it on the drainboard.

'Here, put some of this in your glass,' Art says, raising the pitcher. Bob passes him his glass. The man nearly fills it. Bob sips, exhales hotly. It tastes the way the visible fumes of rubber cement smell.

'Put a little stone in your bone. I thought you college boys were all great drinkers.'

'I'm at school with Alice,' Bob says. He takes another, careful sip. It can be gotten used to. 'A grade behind, actually.'

'Well, it's crap, anyways,' Art says. 'What do you suppose they're teaching you?'

Bob considers what might appeal to a union man before he answers, 'This year we took *The Grapes of Wrath.*'

'Now, that's an interesting example.' Art leans across the table, bringing his face up to Bob's. 'Now you tell me why that's such great literature when it's just a bad book?'

'It's bad?' Bob shakes his head. 'I don't know.'

'It's good guys and bad guys. Don't you see? The landowners are just evil in that book, like they enjoyed it. But they had to get through the day the same as you and me. It's not fair to be so one-sided, and teach that to kids.'

'I think,' Bob says slowly. His head is remarkably clear. 'I think, that when you're attacked by a wild animal, you don't worry about whether or not it's trying to feed its young.' He stands up. The room tips at an angle, very smoothly, as he rises. 'I think I should use the washroom.'

From the hall, he hears Vivian say, 'You should be ashamed of yourself. You only saw the movie, you've never read Steinbeck in your life.'

'I know a bunch of self-important pricks when I see them,' Art says. 'I don't have to read Steinway to know that.'

Anything else is masked by the flushing of the toilet. After,

Bob leaves the house by the front door, rather than pass through the kitchen again, and starts to circle to the backyard. He's in the corridor between houses when he hears Mrs. Porter's voice.

'They're just going away for the weekend, then she's back at school on Monday. I'm not having her be a high-school dropout on top of everything else.' Her voice breaks and someone, man or woman, makes soft, reassuring sounds. Mrs. Porter's voice rises, recovering volume if not strength, and she says, 'If Ted were here to see this, it would kill him.'

Bob stays standing at the corner of the house, hidden by the hedge. The air is warmer here, from the heat collected by the brick walls during the day and now being released. He looks across the depth of the next yard, to the end of Ken's yard, then turns his head slightly. Peripheral vision is more sensitive to motion than a direct stare. He's waiting for the image of Susan, in her white tablecloths, raising her feet in the quick steps of the Monkey, covering the ground between here and there. It's hardly any distance at all.

The Day J. Edgar Hoover Died

DAVE IS YOUNG ENOUGH to want to try everything once, so he takes the jumpseat in the back of the London cab, facing the woman he's met after presenting a letter of introduction from his father's office. He makes a mental note, a reminder to say 'thank you' for the dinner she's taking him to. The woman, Ellen, is in her late forties and works at the American Embassy. Dave is eighteen. It is May, 1972.

'I suppose you don't notice the accents as much,' Ellen says.

'I'm sorry,' Dave leans forward. She's farther away from him than he would have imagined possible in any kind of automobile. There's enough floor space to put down a mattress.

'Well, being Canadian.' She moves her hand flat across the space between them, drawing the border. 'You talk the same way, don't you?'

'We do? *Do* we?' The cab takes a sharp corner. Dave pulls his legs together; the jumpseat is only a small, padded square. He puts his hands down to clutch the edges.

'I'm not sure you're hearing my real voice,' he says. 'I may have picked up some kind of accent in Yugoslavia. I met so many people.' He looks out the window, surprised to see the distance receding rather than approaching. He decides in future to sit facing the front. But now he's able to add *jumpseat, London cab* to the mental list he keeps, of experiences he'll need to draw on as a stage actor. That's his ambition: this summer is a time to collect impressions. At odd moments, his attention is captured completely, as though the rest of the world dims and recedes, and he thinks, This *counts*. The sidestreet in Belgrade, coming back from Troika, returns to him. They'd turned onto a one-way street and had to slow, almost to a stop, behind a street-cleaning machine nearly the width of the road. He presses his wrists against his thighs.

'I haven't met many Canadians,' Ellen admits. 'Your father, of course, when he was here. Other than that –' She makes a slight uplifting of her shoulders. Dave senses no apology in the movement. Unconsciously, he lifts his own shoulders and duplicates the gesture, then catches himself and nods at the window.

'Everything looks like it's been here forever, the way all the space is used. Some of the people, even.' He points, uncertain the angle is right for Ellen to see the two men. Black-robed, they are wearing white wigs above cleanly-shaven faces. Lawyers, he thinks, then corrects himself. Barristers.

'There's at least one of everything in London, that's for sure.'

Ellen leans forward and taps a coin against the window behind the driver. Her skirt rides up, a little over her knees. Dave glances at her hand, to examine the new ten-pence piece. The currency values in Belgrade had confused him. He doubts he could have coped with pounds, shillings, and pence and gives thanks for the new British decimal system.

'Up here,' she says, her voice louder.

Dave feels the cab move laterally towards the curb. He corrects for his weight pulling him forward and to the side by bracing his feet against the floor. His shoes are new, from Florsheim's, and the leather soles don't offer much resistance. By the time he's straightened up, Ellen's paid the cab and opened the door. She's tall, but steps to the curb in a fluid fashion that looks nothing at all like a woman unfolding from a car. Dave crouches and follows her, managing not to hit his head on the top of the door frame.

'I usually hit my head on the door,' he says, touching his temple. 'I've never learned, really, how to get in and out of a car. I like these cabs.'

Ellen is stuffing her wallet back into her purse. She says, 'What?'

'I also fall down at least once during the winter. On patches of ice?' Dave raises his arms in a toned-down version of a man slipping on a smooth surface or a banana peel. The rigid spine and windmilling arms are the same in each case. Body language has a lot of homonyms; physical movement is more finite than what it expresses. A man on the other side of the street turns in his direction and Dave brings his arms down.

'That's the place,' Ellen points to a building a few metres away. He turns. It looks like a glassed-in sidewalk café, an enclosed terrace. Bright white-painted tables and chairs are visible through the window.

Dave steps back to be on the outside of the sidewalk as they walk to the entrance. The evening is warm and clear. The air has a slightly dusty scent. He shifts his vision out of focus for a moment, enjoying the sensation he can actually *see* the air.

The restaurant is called Steamboat Willie's. The name is familiar to Dave, but he doesn't remember what it means until he's inside. Steamboat Willie was the mouse who evolved into Mickey. A young woman with hair the colour of strong tea shows them to a table and offers them menus.

'The girl will come for your order. Meantimes, anything to drink?' she asks, in an accent nothing like Dave's. He looks across the table, to take his cue from Ellen.

'I'm going to have a Martini,' she says. 'Gordon's, if you have it, or Beefeater's.' She turns to Dave, 'I suppose a pint of bitter? Stout?'

'Is that like draft beer? Sure.' He's only just legal to drink at home, and he usually gets carded. 'I'll have that,' he says, and the woman moves away. Dave opens his menu and watches over its top as Ellen lights a cigarette, the flame from a silver lighter touching the end of the Winston for a mere second. She exhales loudly and smooths back her hair with the hand not holding the cigarette. A large blond man two tables away turns in their direction. The table between is empty. Dave puts the menu flat over the service plate. His father is fair, and his hair was thinning, the last time Dave saw him. Dave's mother assures him his own hair will stay as dark and thick as hers.

'Everything looks good,' he says, although he is slightly confused by the cartoon illustrations printed on the pages. They don't seem, to him, very *English*. His hotel in Belgrade, the Metropole, was on one side of a large park, with an old cathedral on the other. In between, the area had a gate topped by an electric sign reading *Dizney Parc*. He'd meant to ask someone what it meant, but the evenings had been taken up reflexively, with no time for such questions.

To Ellen, he says, 'In Yugoslavia, butter was listed with the cheeses, as a side order.'

'Isn't that interesting? Ah.' Ellen reaches up to take her martini from a tray carried by the woman who seated them. The tray tips and Dave reaches up to take his mug quickly, before the balance is upset.

'Thank you,' he says. Then, 'Everything was interesting. In one place the, uh, toilets, were marked with pictures of shoes. I'm getting used to those sort of line drawings of men and women.' He sketches a guitar-figure in the air. 'Even roosters and chickens, or pictures of Henry the Eighth and Anne Boleyn. But shoes?' He shakes his head, then sips his drink. It tastes like beer.

'It's all very educational, isn't it? When it's new.' Ellen smiles. She's quite pretty. 'London won't be quite so different.'

'From Canada?' Dave looks down at his menu. 'Original Mississippi Riverboat Pizza,' he reads out loud. 'I wonder what that is?'

'You could try it.'

'I think I'll have to.' Dave closes his menu.

Ellen does the ordering. She's going to have a small steak. 'Very rare,' she tells the waitress, then explains to Dave, 'Over here that means well done. You'll learn to adjust to these things.'

'Uhm.' Dave moves his forefinger around the rim of his mug. While they wait for their food, she asks to be caught up on his father's affairs. The newsmagazine has moved Don to its Middle East bureau; Tel Aviv is the end of Dave's trip. The travel agent had discovered a cheap flight out of Mirabel. He said, 'A little dog-leg into Old Hugo. Not too painful,' and plans were locked-in. Don would have known someone anywhere in Europe, at any rate, and was at no loss for contacts to show Dave around. That was something to count on, at least, having his name recognized. 'Oh, *Don's* son,' people would say, but they never seemed to be looking directly at Dave when they did. He's not sure just what he's supposed to do, then, what expectation to live up to. After one introduction, for obscure reasons, he heard himself say, 'Every guy is *someone's* son,' and felt a moment's dizziness, as though he'd suddenly become weightless.

Dave doesn't recognize many of the names Ellen inquires after, but his father's life has never been very open to him. He remembers once – he couldn't have been more than eleven or twelve – opening all Don's mail. He started with cautious patience, wanting only to peel off the stamps, but after the first envelope tore, he abandoned restraint and ripped open the rest, leaving the letters on the hall floor when he took the stamps to his room. Dave saw his mother approach his father with the letters, later, but they closed the den door and left him outside. He waited and waited for his punishment. It was his first experience with the seemingly trivial act, the consequence of business not performed centre stage. Now he makes general statements that seem satisfactory to Ellen.

There's a small scuffle at the next table. A man in a beige raincoat has been seated just as the waitress tries to pass with Ellen's steak and Dave's pizza. He bends to retrieve his paper before sitting opposite his coat. The waitress exhales loudly.

'Pizza?'

'Here.' Dave raises his hand. A shallow oval dish is placed in front of him. He looks over at Ellen's steak. It's the size and shape of a hamburger.

'Eat up nice,' Dave hears the waitress say, but she's gone before he asks, 'What?' He can't imagine what else would have sounded like that. Heat a slice? Be kind to mice? He looks across the table, his eyebrows raised.

'In Belgrade,' Ellen says. 'I wondered who took you around.'

'Oh. From the embassy? Perkins, a couple. We went to the American Club my second night and met all kinds of people. I sort of moved with this group. There was an artists' colony. Skardilla? Scaryada? We went there a lot.'

'You didn't meet Nancy Prutain? She's with the magazine. I understood she knew Don quite well.' Ellen dips her knife into a pot of mustard and covers the grey meat with dull yellow.

'Actually, I did.' Dave nods. The man at the next table rustles his newspaper, folding back half of the first page to read the inside column. Dave glances over and reads a headline: FBI Director Dies. 'Look at that,' Dave whispers, angling his head.

Ellen glances over quickly. The headline is upside down to her, but she looks back almost immediately.

'The telex came to the embassy.' Her tone is indecipherable.

'It's about time.' Dave grimaces. 'Maybe now the world is safe for democracy.'

'Don't say that too quickly. There was a time the country needed a strong man like that. People forget what it was like.'

Dave has never in his life heard a good word said about the man; certainly his father never wrote one. But he's been taught to base his opinions on facts, not other opinions, so he says, 'Sorry,' and picks up his fork. The pizza looks like an eye. Inside the white plate, there's a rim of bright orange around a dark centre. Dave touches the centre with his fork and it collapses. The dish is filled with chunks of onion. He cuts to the bottom and raises some to his mouth. The texture and flavour suggest raw biscuit dough. He swallows, then swallows two gulps of his beer.

'You didn't tell me about Nancy,' Ellen says.

'Yes.' Dave rests his fork, tines down, on the edge of the dish. 'I had dinner with a friend of hers, last night. A place called Troika.' He glances down at his pizza and remembers the huge room, thick with the odour of wonderful foods, cigar smoke, and the impressive level of noise. Eskine had kept pouring wine, carefully diluting Dave's with seltzer. Even so, Dave was red-faced and sweating by the time the table was cleared and the dancing started.

'Nancy's friend?' Ellen leans forward across the table. Her eyes are very bright. Dave's heard about the heat of English mustard. 'Is he nice?'

'He was to me,' Dave nods. Against the evidence of the first taste, he decides the pizza can't be that bad, and he takes another mouthful. It's awful, lumpy and metallic, with no chewy bits of melted cheese. He doesn't know what it is, but it's not pizza. Suddenly, being served this seems very unfair and he feels frustrated and filled with rage and about ten years old. His parents were still married to each other when he was ten, and all the difficult choices were made without him. He cools his mouth with the last of the beer before telling Ellen, 'He offered me a scholarship with the Yugoslavian Ballet.'

'A dancer?' Ellen's mouth opens very wide. Dave can see either bits of meat or metal fillings on the chewing surfaces of her back teeth. 'Nancy got herself a dancer after –' Ellen breaks off and laughs, a sound that seems to have more to do with her chest and shoulders than her mouth and throat.

Years from now, Dave will dine out on the story. 'I was offered a scholarship with the Yugoslavian Ballet,' he will tell people. Faces will turn in his direction. He will dip his head, modestly, and qualify, 'The offer was made by a Dutch architect, and he *had* been drinking, but I felt pretty for three days.'

Now he looks at Ellen, damp-eyed above the napkin she has pressed over her mouth. Dave has an impulse to stand quickly, tipping the table to her side. Glass would fall and shatter on the floor. He would say, 'What do you know about it? What do you know about real people and their lives?' Then he would walk away and leave her alone to deal with the mess.

He looks across to the next table. J. Edgar Hoover is dead. He looks down at the inedible pizza in front of him, then back at Ellen. She raises one hand and waves it apologetically. He shrugs, not really focused on her. Some things are more important than others, and he's learning to tell the difference.

Swans and Rabbits

OUR HOUSE, when I was a boy, sat at the low end of a long drive against a retaining wall before the river. Sometimes swans would circle this wall a short distance upstream and cross the narrow lawn to beat alarming tattoos against the cellar door. The kitchen was a floor above, so I could look down and see these creatures, lopsided and ungainly without the smooth buoyancy of water, hear them hissing and trumpeting their frustration at being excluded from the life within.

I'd been told they could break a man's arm with a stroke of the bill. This seemed improbable to me, until one spring day when I was eleven, and watching the dust-coloured mass of cygnets at the end of the wall. A grown swan bobbled and rocked toward me. I stood still. Its walk was audibly flat-footed on the grass. I took a step forward. The swan stopped. I took a second step. The head turned in my direction.

These were not the features of a budgie, or even a duck. I was looking at reptile eyes in a reptile head. The neck feathers were slicked down by river water, into a mail of overlapping scales. The bill barely parted, but the hissing was visible as a wet bubbling. The sound of evil; the look of our stereotype for madness: foaming at the mouth.

I covered my face with my forearms, stepped back into a vertiginous panic. Through the narrow space, I saw the wings spread, large as bedsheets flapping on a clothesline. They beat forward, pushing towards me all the winds on earth. After a tumbling of green, grass, and blue, sky, I looked up from the ground. At twenty paces, the swan sauntered away, twitching its tail feathers, as clumsy and laughable as a Thanksgiving turkey. I rolled over onto my back, not ready to try standing.

Could break a man's arm, I thought. There were things yet to learn.

OUR NEAREST neighbours had always been the Goits, at the top of the drive. Mrs. Goit would come down the drive for mid-morning coffee on weekdays, tipped forward in her high-heeled mules, with a pale woolen cardigan thrown across her shoulders and held secure at the neck, two packages of Marlboros clutched in her other hand. Sometimes she would still be at our place when I got home for lunch, and I would trace lazy eights over the bottom of my bowl of tomato soup, hungry for what I could over-hear from the sun-room beyond the kitchen. I knew that women hushed their voices over important issues, where men would come as close to shouting as they could while maintaining clear enunciation. The lowered voice demanded more of the audi-ence, a straining interest.

Mrs. Goit had married beneath her. This seems to be a mean-ingless concept, now, but then it was thrilling, illicit, with a blood-heating vulgarity. Later, I lifted from my sister's room a school book – *Of Mice and Men* – and, reading how Curly kept one hand in a glove filled with Vaseline, for the sake of his pam-pered wife, I flushed with the same glamour, burned with a sen-sation poorly defined as shame. *Envy* would be closer, I think; envy for such a public declaration of one's hold on another, one's being held. But prurience was the temper of the times, then, rep-utation and ruin were close cousins to be scrutinized for family resemblance. On the same shelf in my sister's room, the cover of a paperback copy of *1984* proclaimed:

A Startling View of Life in 1984
Forbidden Love ... Fear ... Betrayal

Mrs. Goit's confidence was not that her marriage had ruined her life. Rather, her life was ruining her marriage. Her money had paid for the house; an unheard-of thing, a wife providing the trappings of success. Details of voting stock, irrevocable trusts, signing authority; these drifted into the kitchen where I sat, meaningless until the wallop of the punch line.

'I'll put the whole damn thing on the block. They have lawyers to manage these things. I don't have the time, when I could be with Frank.'

And then my mother's voice, soothing as a cool hand. Sometimes, after Mrs. Goit had left, she would stand in front of the sink for long minutes, running warm water over the tea cup she turned over and over until it squeaked against her skin. She would smile the way she smiled in the car, Sundays, when the time before us, like the highway, stretched forward without limits, endless.

On these excursions, my sister and I would bounce in the back seat, bored to distraction with each other's company, and making our plight worse with numbing repetitions of the Cow Joke.

'There's a bunch of cows.'

'Herd.'

'Heard what?'

'Herd of cows.'

'Of course I've heard of cows.'

'No. A cow herd.'

'So what? I have no secrets from cows. There's another bunch.'

'Herd.'

'Heard what?'

And on and on, until mother heard peckishness, if not murderous intent, in our voices and suggested stopping for a snack.

'Just park in a field,' I said. 'We can let Debra out to *graze.*' At thirteen, my sister had achieved a generous co-existence between her baby fat and the pudgy suggestion of new swellings, the shape of things to come.

'That's enough, Bren,' my father said. We stopped at a road-side stand for steamed hot dogs in soggy rolls and thick-cut chips fried in a viscous, amber solution. It was from there, on the dirt shoulder of the highway, that my mother saw the hand-printed signs: PICK YOUR OWN. BASKETS PROVIDED.

'Blueberries,' she said, as though the word were sacred; she had unexpected enthusiasms. 'Oh, Eric, it'll be fun.'

We laboured in the fields under the mid-day sun. At least, three of us did. 'I'm not dressed for this,' Debra said, and she stood in her ruffled blouse and full skirt, white socks and pumps, eating berries from the bushes closest to the trail. 'If she's not picking, she shouldn't be eating,' I protested, but the response was a typical, 'Leave your sister alone.'

Bushels, I estimated. Pecks and acres. Some large measure was needed to describe the harvest in woven-lathing baskets in the car's back seat. It was usual, on the return trips, for me the lie on the floor, my feet on Debra's side, my belly arched up over the universal axle.

I read comics hoarded during the week, forbidden on school nights. I lay in the dust and fumes of the car floor, the highway bare inches below that, and coveted the Torch's incredible, 'Flame on!' There was a soothing, hypnotic pulse deep in my middle ear, from the vibrations. And more, that day, a rhythmic, liquid sound. I nodded, keeping time, until the images in front of me blurred, and I was ready to put my head over my arms and sleep. At that moment, my mother's voice cut through my lethargy.

'Debra! What have you done?'

There was a terrible, wet noise. The back of my head was shockingly hot, all in an instant, as surprising as can be a sudden burning, through your winter coat, after you've been leaning for some time against the radiator in a public building. My eyes closed. The car rocked underneath me, in a crazy loop, and then there was fresh air, light, and my father's hands pulling me from the car. I recognized the bland, starchy scent of his handkerchief, pressed up against my face, felt the rough scrubbings, and then was able to open my eyes, and see my mother, off the side of the road, performing a similar action on Debra. I looked into the car. There was a large pool, deep purple, with a shrinking outline of where my body had been on the floor. On the seat, on my side, the wooden baskets were cleaned to the bottom slats.

'Jesus Christ!' I swore aloud, for the first time in my father's presence. 'She ate all the berries and puked on my head.'

I HAVE AN aerogramme from Debra, dated three years back. After her divorce, she set off to travel in the Far East, and I would get these bulletins, whenever something happened she thought I might enjoy. My own marriage was wobbly at this time, without an intrinsic direction. My wife insisted this was no tragedy, our slow drift towards separation.

'We should have been related by blood,' Linda said, 'not marriage. We'll be good friends, what we should have been all along.' I agreed and disagreed, and she took a sublet from a friend of hers, a dancer with a four-month road tour. Debra said, tragedy or no, 'It means you got an F in Marriage. I've signed up for a different course, Independent Travel. You should do something for yourself. Take a chance on something new.' But I couldn't, at the time, so I allowed myself the entertainment of her life, second-hand.

The paper is pale blue and flimsy. Her handwriting is cramped, to get the whole story into the limited space.

In Nepal, she hired a car and driver to take her up the mountainside to a temple recommended as a 'must see' by someone she left nameless. Through some mix-up in language, in understanding, what she got was a man in uniform, a black limousine. So she sat, in solitary splendor, while the chauffeur navigated the treacherous, serpentine mountain road. Their progress was slow enough for word to spread about the *mem s'ab* in the long black car, and a procession formed in her wake.

You can't imagine the heat, she wrote. *The car circled and circled. Faces were pushed up to the windows. There was a lot of noise, excited chatter, palms held out and fingers pointing. Round and round we went. I'd anticipated a long trip and had a big breakfast at the hotel – melon, and a kind of heavy grain bread, fruit juice and tea. Round and round we went. Finally, we arrived at the temple. I opened the car door, to a blast of air like a hot brick. The crowd pushed closer. I leaned forward and tossed my breakfast out at their feet. I pulled the door closed and asked the driver to take me back to my hotel.*

I phoned Linda, to share the story. She always liked Debra. There was a pause, when I finished reading the letter, and I spoke quickly, to maintain the connection. My voice echoed back to me through the receiver.

'Do you suppose they'll build a temple annex? A smaller shrine to the Goddess of Recently Eaten Food?' That made me laugh, makes me laugh still.

'No, Bren,' Linda said. 'Women aren't goddesses. It's a nice story, but you have to change your thinking about what things mean.'

I'd heard that before. Only a week earlier, after she'd agreed to meet me for lunch in neutral, public, territory, she'd listened, rebutted, listened, and finally, at the exact moment of one of those total silences that fall over restaurants, she'd raised her voice to command, 'Worship *God*. Venerate the *dead*. Leave *me* alone.'

I ended the conversation, broke open my sourdough loaf and spread butter over the warm softness of its insides. The knife-handle was cool against my palm. My hands are soft, unscarred by hard labour. One knuckle carries the mark of a deep rope-burn, but that was acquired sailing, in a careless movement.

'IT'S FRANK'S new hobby,' Mrs. Goit said. 'But I thought you would like to see these.' She was taking Debra and me to the out-building at the end of her property. This would be a 'carriage house' now, but she called it the garage. She swung open the heavy double doors and we stepped into the twilight gloom. The window at the far end was smudged with grease and allowed only a grey, wintry illumination. It took a moment for my eyes to adjust, and then they widened to accommodate my rapture.

'Rabbits!'

And so there were – from low cages fronted with chicken wire, six, seven, eight rabbits placidly returned my stare. When I first heard the word *herbivore*, without knowing what it meant, I knew I would approve of what it described. The rabbits chewed processed kibble, their split lips puffed out like cheeks. One stopped to wash its face, pulling its ear down with a front paw. I wanted to clutch the front of my pants, run in circles screaming, slap myself in the face – anything to dilute my smothering joy. Instead, I asked if they had names. Personalizing the world was important.

'Frank named them, yes. I'm not sure I can remember them all. Let's see.' And pointing at each cage in turn, she rhymed off, 'Whitey, Boots, Shadow, Queenie, Sapphire, Pinky, Opal and Miss Charlotte.' She laughed at that, the last name, and gave my sister a complicit look. Debra nodded wisely. She had turned fourteen, and was a 'standing' at the New Mode Beauty Shoppe, a common enough occurrence, judging by the photographs in her high school year book. Like her teen-aged contemporaries in 1961, Debra looked to be about forty years old.

I had to promise not to visit the garage without first receiving permission from the Goits and, although I chafed at the suggestion that I was irresponsible, any threat to the rabbits, I gave my word.

On the way home, I made a mistake and quoted to my sister, 'Tell me about the rabbits, George.' Debra grabbed my arm and pinched, hard, the soft skin on the inside of my elbow.

'Stay out my room,' she said. 'If I catch you reading my books again I'll kill you in your sleep.'

I danced out of her reach, effectively threatened. It was not death, my concern – that had no real meaning to me – but the idea of missing such an event, being killed *in my sleep*.

LATE IN THE evenings, I read the newspaper, inured by sleeplessness against the descriptions of a world where madness is distanced only by the remoteness of the datelines. I was doing this, idly letting my eyes drop from column to column, scanning fragments before moving on, when I saw the obituary for Mr. Goit. Hardly a common surname, and the notice mentioned he was predeceased by his loving wife, Charlotte. There was a time and place for the memorial service, and a wish that expressions of sympathy be in the form of contributions to the Cancer Society.

I folded the paper neatly into sixths, leaving the obituary face-up on the coffee table, so I would see it in the morning. Lately I seem to forget how things end; the resolutions of novels, conclusions of television movies, the last few minutes of each day. Linda has told me that this is no new development, no symptom of progressive weakness.

'You don't forget,' she said. 'You just don't accept that things finish. In your world everything goes on and on, forever and ever, amen. Well, that's not a life, Bren, that's a life sentence.' I must have clamped my hand over the space between my heart and left shoulder – I had a bruise there the next day, a bruise that took weeks to fade – and she added, 'I'm sorry. I shouldn't have said that. I'll come back for the rest of my stuff some other time. We can't discuss anything now.' She did ask, on her way out, 'You'll be all right?'

'Me?' I looked up, as the door closed behind her, then I sat surrounded by the neat piles she had made of her possessions, her personal accumulations. Her copy of *1984* was on top of a stack of books. The cover blurb read: 'Orwell's Prophetic View of the Future.'

The year itself had come and gone.

I WAS TEMPTED to ask, 'Was it a good passing?' when Mrs. Hogg, Frank Goit's sister, ushered me into the reception room at Beechwood. Instead, I murmured the vague phrases about sorrow and loss, keeping my voice low to preclude having to construct a whole sentence.

She leaned towards me. 'So you knew him well?'

'My parents did,' I said, and told her who they were, that they were retired now, in Kelowna. 'But I remember them, your brother and his wife.' Then I wondered if I should have prefaced the nouns with 'late'.

'I think I remember your family now,' she said, stepping back to look at me straight on, up and down. 'Brendan, an odd name for a boy. You had a sister. Older, wasn't she?'

'Was, and still is,' I said. 'She's out of the country, now, but I'm sure she'd want me to express her condolences.'

'Oh, I've always wanted to see the world. Tell me, where has she been, where is she going next?'

We had crossed the room while talking. Mrs. Hogg was seated in a chair with a wooden back and a green velvet cushion. I looked down at her, her interest honest and visible, and I lied with an unrehearsed fluency.

'She's in Nepal. She has no other immediate plans.'

'It's different, now, isn't it, for the young people? They want to go, and they can just pack up and be gone.' She raised one hand and walked two fingers across the air. Then she folded both hands in her lap. 'I don't know if I envy them or not, all that freedom.'

'No.' I shook my head. 'No, don't envy her.'

'I WOULDN'T FLY to Nepal, no,' the man said. 'It's an expensive trip, and you're unlikely to accomplish anything.' His office, in the External Affairs building, had the matte of fading newness, rather than the patina of use, the gloss of restoration. 'You might not be allowed to see her.'

The consul had his hand over a file folder on his desk, the slim record of Debra's arrest and conviction. The buff cardboard was crisp, unthumbed. The consul's nails were manicured.

'Not see her?' I repeated. 'My sister? Aren't there laws?' Phrases from forgotten sources came to me, and I slid them across the desk, hoping they might scald that hand. 'The Geneva Convention. The Warsaw Pact.'

The man looked around the room quickly, then leaned across his desk towards me. His voice, when he spoke, was low but exact.

'There are times, in these drug cases, when we can demand extradition and insist on our own legal process for the offenders.

And sometimes the offenders get away from us at the airport in Montreal. I know you won't repeat this, okay?'

'Yes.' I put my own hands, the light touch of my fingertips, over the desktop on my side, as though it were a Ouija board, and waited for a revelation of the future. I kept my eyes down. You have to make an effort not to influence the outcome, that's one of the rules.

'We tried that. Your sister has no record, after all. And she's a woman of considerable means. Where's her motive?'

I shrugged, managing not to lift my hands from the desk. The consul opened the file. He read from the first page, or the only page; in either case, no sheet was pushed to the side, or creased over the top of the folder. He might have known what he had to say, and needed the moment to prepare himself.

'Debra was seen in the company of a man under surveillance by the Nepalese authorities. I can't give you his name, but he's an expatriated Swiss. No evident means of support.' The consul looked up at a corner of the room, 'Well, Swiss,' then back at me. 'They're insisting on this connection, which effectively takes the case out of our hands. She, your sister, has refused to give any testimony against him.'

I stood up and moved away from my chair. My trouser legs dropped down from where they had wrinkled behind my knees. He also stood, after closing the file folder. It was only then that I noticed it was labelled with her other name, the surname of the man she had married and divorced.

'Thank you,' I said. 'For your time, and the effort you've made. I think I understand now.' After a moment I remembered to extend my hand.

'You do?' His handshake was strong, his skin the same temperature as mine. He was wearing his watch on the right wrist, its face inward. 'Of course we'll be in touch with you, if there're any new developments.' He paused, and his tone altered. 'Does any of this make sense to you?'

'No, not really,' I said. 'But I think I understand.'

WHEN I WAS twelve, Mrs. Goit was briefly hospitalized with what was called 'female problems.' I think, now, her condition was not cystitis, ovarian cysts, vaginal prolapse; not one of these topics of conversation trotted out for discussion at the dinner parties I attend. I think, now, her condition would be referred to as 'a breakdown,' not yet suitable as table-talk. Not yet. I think she tried to commit suicide.

I remember a morning when I was wakened by a metallic, crashing sound, followed by a rumble like distant thunder. Then, again; a sequence. The image I constructed, plausible enough, was of someone trying to carry the clothes dryer up the cellar stairs, dropping the weight on each step, shaking the house. The reality, however, was that a Public Works crew was blasting the iced-over river, to prevent flooding later in the spring, when the tons of melted water could swell over the retaining wall.

I remember an evening when the ambulance was at the top of the drive. Its interior was lit like a refrigerator. This was less bright than the pulse of the roof light cutting ripples over the asphalt surface between the Goits' house and where I stood. When the attendants rolled the gurney to the back of the ambulance, their shirts changed colour, by a trick of perception, from brown to pale blue. The sheet over Mrs. Goit changed from red to white.

I don't remember if those events, the blasting and the breakdown, were in the same year. My mother may have been worried about flooding, or about Mrs. Goit alone on a Friday night (Frank was out of town; no explanation), when she asked Mrs. Goit to sit with us. We were far too old to need that attention, although we were young enough to fail at learning the nuances of three-handed bridge. If there were rules at all, they were like Debra's rules for Monopoly, seeming to change with each game. Mrs. Goit pronounced us 'Tits on a goose,' breaking the tension I was afraid would make me cry.

'Okay,' she said. 'If you can't play cards, I'll read them for you.'

There was an elaborate lay-out, cards crossed over cards, a line of four face-down to one side, a complicated litany of relationship. 'Hope crosses Life,' I recall, and, 'Journey takes away Fortune.'

Debra and I, it seemed, had plodding, routine futures. I would not be gunned down in a saloon, which had been one of my major aspirations; Debra would not be a prima ballerina, although she would graduate from high school.

'Now do yours,' my sister suggested. I wonder if she was hoping for a standard, something to compare to her own fate?

'You can't do your own.' Mrs. Goit shuffled the cards together, put the deck beside her cup and saucer.

'I'll do it.'

The cards were warm in my hands, slightly greasy. I shuffled in that clumsy, amateur manner, lifting sections from the middle, dropping them to the back. Then I laid out four, face down, like the quarter-markings of a clock.

'This is a different way,' I said, as I flipped over the first card, a black jack. 'A man,' I nodded. The second card, at three o'clock, was the queen of hearts. 'A woman.' I was starting to feel a tightening in the muscles of my face, the mask that fixes my features in situations when I find, a new shock every time, that I have called attention to myself. I quickly flipped over the third card, trying to remember how Mrs. Goit had strung together vague phrases, portentous and meaningless at the same time. The card was the six of diamonds.

I started speaking quickly, trying to get the words out so I could also be audience to them. They were unplanned, careless.

'The spades mean the man has gone on a trip, walking over the ground inside of digging in it. The queen is a woman at home, and the hearts mean she is waiting for the man to come back. The six means,' I took a deep breath. Then, 'Rabbits. The queen has had six rabbits.'

Mrs. Goit was not looking at me, nor at the cards. She looked across the table, at Debra, who was staring down at the cards. I was sufficiently removed as centre of attention to casually flip over the last card. Hardly glancing at it, the five of spades, I added, 'This happened Tuesday.'

Debra looked up, then, into Mrs. Goit's stare. By some signal, invisible to me, they both stood and left the room, stood whispering in the hall outside the kitchen. Alone at the table, I might have memorized my posture, my state of mind. The attitude would return to me, again and again, as a man held hostage to a restaurant table, between presentation of the cheque and the return of a credit card, while Linda 'freshened up.' It is a recondite time, that.

The television went on in the family room before Debra returned to the kitchen, without Mrs. Goit.

'She thought I told you.'

'Told me what?' At this point, no longer abandoned, I was able to start kicking the leg of the table.

'One of the rabbits had babies. Mrs. Goit calls them kittens.'

'Babies!' I drummed harder against the tableleg. 'Can we go see?'

'That's just it. She didn't want you to know. Because you can't see them. She says if you bother them now the mother will kill them.'

'No,' I said, too angry to raise my voice. 'That's not true. It's not fair.'

But I had stopped believing, some time earlier, that the world was fair and I knew, or would remember knowing, what my sister said was true. I would never see the young rabbits, no matter how much I cared to, no matter how gentle I was, because the risk was too great. No matter how strong my desire, it was puny and worthless against the instinct of the rabbits, the thing that Mrs. Goit knew – what we call love – how it is exclusive and protective, and will choose nothing over less.

I sat at the table, in the harsh, domestic light of the kitchen, and spread the cards over the table once more. 'It was just a trick,' I said. Outside, the river ice was melting too quickly, and the water level was rising. There was a major flood, either that year or the next.

Domestic Order

KEN KEEPS HIS EYES focused on a spot about the size of a host, consecrated or not, on his father's chest; the suction pad of the cardiac monitor. During his last complete physical, Ken lay on a cold metal table with these clinging to his own chest, his upper arms, his calves, their slight tugging exactly the sensation of being nibbled by fish.

Sympathetic goosebumps had broken out on his flesh and he imagined his lips turning blue, his mother's voice calling him from the lake. He would be eleven in this memory, standing knee-deep in the water, looking down at his feet on the silt bottom, unable to lean forward into the most rudimentary dog paddle. That winter he was signed up for swimming lessons after school – sometimes his wet hair would freeze into a sharp bear claw against the back of his neck as he waited for the bus home – and the following spring the instructor from the Y, and Ken's mother, moved to another town. Ken never conquered his fear, of water closing over his head. He was afraid he would be effaced.

'Could you spell your last name for me?' the technician had asked.

Since his surname is not a difficult one, Ken assumed he was being given a rote task to put him at ease, to keep the EKG from recording the indulgence of mortal speculation rather than the placid pumping of his everyday heart.

'Capital em,' he started, and rhymed off the letters in a sing-song. To his surprise, the technician copied this down, and he realized she had needed the information. There was no deeper purpose. He, once again, had read too much into the situation.

The oxygen tent is made of a plastic about six times the thickness of a dry cleaning bag. Through this, his father's skin has the hazy cast of meat with freezer burn. Meat wrapped in plastic sweats and loses all its moisture: this is something Ken knows:

aluminum foil is best for long-term preservation. He considers the logistics of getting his father into pajamas. He always wore them at home, and kept his slippers at the side of the bed precisely where his feet would touch down in case of a fire. Domestic order is everything.

In the silence of Intensive Care, the tent makes an icy, crackling sound. 'The nurse says you're comfortable,' Ken whispers in the direction of his father's chest. The bed is cranked up to prevent fluid collection in the lungs. Ken thinks of doughnuts dunked in coffee, the sacs and pockets of air filling with liquid, the spreading stain as the doughy connecting tissue is saturated. They would be almost eye-to-eye, he and his father, if he turned. He puts his hands deep into his pockets and, louder, adds, 'I don't know how they can tell a thing like that. I guess it's relative.'

'Your son is visiting,' the day nurse says from the doorway. Earlier, in the hall, Ken had hesitated to make any assumptions, and checked the man's plastic name bar for professional initials. A white costume could mean anything. The man might have been, even, a barber, hired to spruce up the critical cases. But Julian Snuggs is an R.N. His voice is loud and artificially bright, like a movie soundtrack in the afternoon when the volume hasn't been turned down to compensate for the hollowness of a nearly-empty theatre. 'Has he said "hello"?'

Ken looks up at his father's face, where a thick X of white adhesive tape marks the goal of a clear plastic tube. An end of this, or another tube entirely, curves up between his eyebrows, a horn more transparent than fingernails, capped by a threaded yellow button. An entry? An exit? It looks careless, the second tube, like something dangling from a dresser drawer after a hasty clean-up. His father's eyes are open and empty, devoid of expression. What looks troubled and thoughtful is merely a reflection of the room's window. Thin grey clouds are weaving over the sky, promising rain. It's Thanksgiving. The tent crackles up and falls.

'Can he talk?' Ken asks, without turning his head, hardly

moving his lips, the way the uncomfortably rich address the hired help. There is no pleasure in counting on the paid kindness of strangers.

'Not speech, with the tube,' the nurse says. 'But he could show that he knows you are here. Has he done that?'

Ken grips the chrome crib-rail of the narrow bed and rocks back on his heels as if preparing to climb up onto the mattress; a six-year-old, bored with the Saturday cartoons and wanting Daddy's attention. It seems to him, now, he's been doing this his whole life. He puts his hands back into his pockets. He can lose awareness of them – his hands and feet – where they are in relation to his body. One night he had awakened with a cold, cold hand touching his face. His own hand, it turned out, numbed by the weight of his head held awkwardly in the v of his arm; but for a moment he had thought, 'Time's up,' and came close to humiliating himself.

'My brother will be here this afternoon,' he says.

'Won't that be nice,' Julian says. He folds the tent back under itself, across the man's chest, and raises the arm where a network of veins map to a border of white – more adhesive tape – and emerge as a clear tunnel to a suspended bottle. The sheet falls back and Ken is staring at his father's cock, thumbing from a Brillo tangle of greyed hair. The circumcision ridge is a leathery brown. With a practised flip, Julian returns the sheet and smooths it down.

So, Ken thinks. Now I know.

Guilty, he looks away, to the cardiac monitor where a line as pale and ephemeral as cigarette smoke suddenly spikes across the cathode tube. What excitement of the heart is being traced? Even here, there can be secrets. The machines are godless; they know nothing immaterial.

'I'll have to come back in a few minutes, to do an irrigation,' Julian says. Ken feels obliged to pretend he understands this, and nods his acceptance. 'But you can visit until then. It's important for him to stay aware of his surroundings.'

'Sure, I'll stay,' Ken agrees. His voice has risen, in pitch and volume, to match the nurse. Overheard, they might be old friends, reunited and attempting to dismiss their new environment, more comfortable in the smooth geography of their memories.

He waits for the nurse to leave, gives him time to get down the hall away from the room. Carefully lifting the edge of the oxygen tent, exposing the side of his father's head, he bends so his lips are close to the man's ear and hisses, 'Damn you. You don't even know I'm here. Damn you to hell.'

He replaces the plastic, trapping the invisible gas, and leaves the room without turning back. The harsh lighting and slick tile of the hospital corridor reminds him of an airport. People come and go.

'WHAT? Am I missing something?' Tony calls from the bathroom.

'Nothing. Never mind.' Ken raises his voice so his brother can hear him through the closed door. He's smoking up in there. 'Smoking out,' Ken calls it, disliking the clubbiness of stoned people, their attitude that sharing the experience made it authentic. Also, he thinks the actual smoking is messy and unattractive. He remembers having joints explode in his fingers, sending showers of embers down to burn his shirt front. 'Wow, seeds,' was the correct response when this happened, delivered with an appreciative nodding. Seeds were organic, an earthy, natural element prized by a group of people who had just scarfed down six family-sized bags of Cheez Doodles. For a time, Ken had thought orange lips were a side effect of marijuana. This theory had caused him considerable alarm when he noticed the number of small children evidently on drugs outside the street's 7-Eleven store. Now he knows better. Some of his friends still smoke in his house – Ken doesn't ask them to respect the difference between a joint or two and the forty to fifty cigarettes he goes through in a day – but the rules are different for family.

He imagines his father will have been given morphine or Demerol. (He knows these words from a required course in

Psychopharmacology: his degree is in Psychology: he also knows the effect of damage caused by a massive insult to the brain. 'Insult to the brain' he reacts to with an emotional and visceral chilling.) For today, at least, drugs will be one more thing for Tony and his father to have in common. Maybe the two of them will giggle and snort, suffixing incomplete statements with 'far out' while Ken slowly transforms himself into a piece of the wall. Being fair helps. Ken's hair is, in fact, the colour of aged ecru semi-gloss; his eyes a pale blue almost transparent in some lights.

'All clean,' Tony announces, entering the room with his hands held up at chest level, palms facing in. They were raised to the euphemism of excusing themselves to 'wash my hands.' Their mother, in a family of men, had lost patience with announcements of 'gotta take a leak.' Ken's private fantasy is that her new husband is attractive to her because, except for first thing in the morning, under cover of the running shower, he never used the toilet at home; he pissed in the pool at work. Years after being abandoned, this mild rudeness still gives Ken a small pleasure.

'Ready to go?' Ken asks. Tony has started a slow orbit of the living room, picking up things for a casual appraisal, putting them back in not quite the right place. 'Put that down,' Ken cautions of an especially fragile ceramic.

'Well, okay,' Tony says. 'Don't fuss. Can I put on a record, at least, or do you get antsy about other people using anything of yours?'

'Go ahead,' Ken says, feeling his brother has narrowly escaped having his hands slapped and willing to be generous. He puts his own hands between his thighs and squeezes his legs closed. 'If you think you have time,' he adds.

'Lots of time, lots of time,' Tony mutters. He's pulling albums half-way out of the teak stand, checking the titles, sliding them back in.

'These are in alphabetical order, aren't they?'

'I'm surprised you could tell,' Ken says after a moment,

needing the time to separate anger from the prissiness he's been accused of. Tony is in his third year of something called 'International Media', a discipline just under Art History and Film Studies on Ken's hierarchy of useless subjects. Their father had curled his lip at Ken's major. 'Just sitting there listening to people making too much of themselves. What kind of thing is that for a man to do? Talk never solved anything.' The man was holding a small knife and an orange, his wrists pressed hard against the table edge to steady his hands, and while he spoke he carefully unwound the skin in a single ribbon that kept the shape of the orange when he put it down on the table. 'It's not just talking,' Ken said. 'It's understanding.' He carefully rolled the bright globe into his palm, its cut latitudes marked by the paler insides. Zest of orange, he thought, just as his father said, 'It's a Jew thing to do.' In Ken's palm the orange was a weightless and vivid as an egg blown and dyed for Easter. Talk never solved anything.

THE NOISY chewing of the coffee grinder drowns out whatever album Tony has chosen. Ken is comfortable in his own kitchen, playing host. He scoops the coffee, fine as flour, from the grinder and into the paper cone filter, slowly pours simmering water over this. A trick of the wrist, the correct pouring technique. While the coffee drips, he puts two mugs and a small pitcher of cream on a plastic tray stamped with a map of the London subway system. He had driven a rented car, on his last holiday, away from London, to Salisbury, to Clovelly, to Land's End. At Glastonbury, Ken walked around the brick outline of the abbey that had once stood there. Only sections of the wall remained, like a theatrical set, the rest dismantled, the stone carted away. The grass under his feet was very green. The brick was grey. Ken looked up, at a leafy tree in the middle distance. A bird cut across his peripheral vision, right at that moment, and disappeared in the sky. Ken looked at his feet again, and understood that King Arthur was buried there. Nobody made this up. He could have left, walked away at any speed, and this would not change. King

Arthur. At that moment, Ken knew the mechanism of history: what was, is.

He bends slightly, his elbows on the Formica counter, to examine his face in the chrome side of the toaster: clear skin, nose a bit round at the end, good upper teeth. Turning his head, straining to see himself in profile, he grimaces, pulling his lower lip down from his teeth, tautening the jaw and chin line he shares with Tony. They are, visibly, brothers; sons of the same father. He lets his face slacken, the crescent of skin where neck meets face creased from too many nights of reading in bed, his head nearly parallel with the book in his lap, almost perpendicular to his body.

Lifting the plastic filter holder from the top of the coffee pot, he swings this over to the sink, one palm cupped to catch any drips, then places it where it will drain directly into the pipe and not stain the porcelain. He carries the tray up the steps, one, two, to the false floor of the living room. When he bought the house the original hardwood had been hidden under wall-to-wall avocado pile held down by a few thousand finishing nails. A rented sander was torn up by eight or twelve hundred of these before Ken admitted defeat and built over the floor.

Tony has his back to the room, staring out the window at the light sprinkling of rain. Against the glass, he looks like one of the black cardboard silhouettes in a shooting gallery. Ken has a flashing, brief image of his brother buckling forward, falling into the room, neatly bent at the waist.

'Coffee's here,' he shouts. Then he adds, 'Maybe you could turn that down?' although the Springsteen album – *Nebraska* – is playing well within his own decibel level.

'The neighbours?' Tony suggests, but he moves to adjust the volume, his fingers slender and elegant on the aluminum knob, his calibration of reduction exact.

'No, me.' Ken stares at his brother, for just a little longer than it takes to acknowledge the diminished sound, then passes him one of the mugs, already creamed. 'You don't take sugar, do you?'

'I don't think I even know anyone who still does.' Tony carries his coffee across the room and sits on the bare floor, leaning against the wall between the stereo speakers. He closes his eyes and a tremor ripples his shoulders as a bass note rolls into the room. 'Excellent,' he says.

'I think you'd hear it better in front of the speakers,' Ken says. His mug is too hot to pick up; he cages his fingers over its rim, the steam rising into his palm, beading into the lines there.

'You be the audience,' Tony offers. 'I'll be on stage.'

'Just like old times.'

'What?' Tony opens his eyes, puts his coffee on the floor beside him. 'Are you going to start that stuff about your being the whipping boy so I could have an idyllic childhood? Are you?'

'I wasn't planning to.' Ken takes an eye-watering sip of his coffee, reaches for a cigarette, coughs into his fist after getting one lit.

'You know what I was thinking about, when I was in your john? Tony the Pony.' He says this with the certainty that his brother will know what he's talking about.

'Tony the Pony?' Ken repeats, then remembers, just before Christmas, maybe a dozen years ago, the ads for a half-sized plastic pony, saddled and frozen in a galloping stance. 'The real riding pony,' a part of the jingle comes back to him. 'God, that's going back a bit,' he says.

'It's like yesterday,' Tony says. 'I wanted one of those more than anything in the whole world. More than,' he pauses, searching for a standard. 'World peace, even.'

'That's some wanting.' Ken glances at his watch. Even immediate family are barred from Intensive Care at mealtimes. It's getting close. He sits, silent, watching his brother. Tony's eyes are closed again. The album ends and the tone arm is raised, mechanically, and swings over to its cradle.

'That *the* bothered me a bit. It should have been apostrophe ess.' He draws this in the air with his next-to-little finger. 'Tony's pony. It was made for me. I watched TV shows I hated – Huckleberry Hound, Quick Draw McGraw – because I knew they would run the commercial. Finally they arrived at Toyland, maybe six of them, a little corral of Tony's ponies. I may have imagined this part, but each of them had a slightly different expression. One was raring to go, one was a work horse; the one I wanted was courageous and resourceful. Yup, he was really something.

'The commercials never mentioned the battery,' he goes on. 'Was I ever that young? It was a big sucker, the size of a car battery.' Tony's hands are T-squares, blocking off a measure in the air before him. 'You know how Dad was. "You don't want a toy that spends money." But I figured even that wasn't insurmountable and I dragged him to Toyland to see it. Tony's pony.'

The light from the window is fading, the single lamp at Ken's side is yellow and weak. He can hardly see his brother across the room, at the end of the parallel strips of flooring, his hands and face amorphous.

'Tony?'

'Oh, he made all the right noises, he said it was nice, and I rode one – the work horse one, not mine – around the floor, while he looked over the book. Warranty? Instructions? I don't know. But he found what he was looking for.'

'Yes.' Ken agrees.

'This little print said Tony could carry up to one hundred and fifty pounds, no more. "You don't want that," he said. "You'll outgrow it by summer, just when you'll want to take it outside." And that was that. End of discussion.'

'You think he should have got it for you?'

'Yes,' Tony says. 'No, not really. What started this was your bathroom scales. Do you know what I weigh?'

'No.'

'One hundred and forty-six pounds. I am twenty-two years old, five foot ten, and I weigh one hundred and forty-six pounds.'

'And you feel that he lied to you?' Ken suggests. His tone is professional. This is not a small story that he's hearing: his working day is predicated on these perceptions tangling in complex warps and wefts: the stories of his own life are neither greater nor less important.

Tony has his head down when he says, 'I would have ridden off into the sunset.' Or perhaps he says, 'I always wanted to have a pet.'

'I'm sorry?' Ken angles his head. There is a low humming from the speakers. The stereo may not be properly grounded. In the manual the leads were red and black; in real life the leads were black and grey. Ken worked on the assumption that the black remained constant. His chances were fifty-fifty.

'I said, So don't tell me.'

'I won't,' Ken says. The small amount of coffee remaining in his mug is cold. He doesn't remember taking more than the one sip; a kind of automatic pilot must have taken over to deal with such an easy activity, drinking coffee. 'What I will tell you is that you've missed visiting time. You're not allowed in for meals. Do you suppose they're messy?'

'What?' Tony asks. Then, 'I'm getting hungry, myself.'

'We could go out. Thanksgiving dinner.'

'Tom turkey and all the trimmings? We'd have to go to the bus station, someplace like that, filled with transients.'

'I was thinking of Hoagy Heaven. We can have turkey subs.'

'The content without the form,' Tony says, and scuttles forward across the floor, pulling himself with his heels towards the sound of Ken's laugh. 'Am I funny?'

'That was.' Ken is dialling up the rheostat for the overhead lights. Tony covers his eyes dramatically, moaning, 'King of the Mole People.'

'I'm going to change. Why don't you listen to the other side of the album? Have some more coffee.'

IN HIS BEDROOM, he pulls himself across the mattress, turns to lie on his back, his ankles crossed, his arms out straight from his shoulders. His hands and feet are suspended over empty space. After the tests at the clinic, for his physical, he had gone to his own doctor's office for the results. His chest x-rays were clipped to a lit viewing screen, two grey gumdrop shapes just over the doctor's right shoulder. 'Difficulties with motor co-ordination? Speech, use of hands, walking?' the doctor asked, ready to check the appropriate boxes on the Family History form, in the column beside the one where 'Maternal' had a ballpoint stroke oblique from left to right. Ken nodded, swallowed, said, 'Yes. Yes.' Only when he was leaving the office did he ask about the x-rays.

'Oh, they're okay. No signs of bronchial malignancies,' the doctor said, 'yet.'

Ken covers his eyes with his forearm. Through the floor-boards, faintly, he can hear Springsteen. Tony has turned up the volume again. He rolls off the bed, steps out of his slacks, changes into jeans and pulls a cotton v-neck over his shirt. Back in the living room, he notes that Tony has achieved, predictably, the wall-hugging stage of expanded consciousness.

'I shouldn't smoke,' Tony says. 'It just makes me depressed.'

'Does it? Then you're right, you shouldn't.' Ken puts his boots beside the couch, takes the tray, his mug, the creamer, crosses to pick up Tony's mug from the floor.

'From now on,' Tony raises his hand in a Scout's promise. 'Cocaine or amphetamines only. This album is so sad. It should be faster.'

Ken, on his way to the kitchen, turns back. 'There's a pitch control on the turntable. You can make it faster.'

'Is that what it's for?' Tony smacks his forehead with his palm, whistles a thin, jagged note. 'What a feature.'

'It's not what it's for, but it'll work. Then we leave, okay?' The question goes unanswered; Tony is bent over the stereo, compromising the speed of sound.

THE SIDEWALK is dry, as if it had never rained. Since he bought a house – is buying his house – Ken has started noticing just how much happens outside of it. He had imagined his universe would become centred, that everything would happen within his own four walls. Instead, it now seems he has to leave home to get experience, excitement, change of any kind. In a single evening he can be two people: the flushed, high-spirited dinner companion; and later the domestic, routine partner, in the tangle of his own sheets, as if his own room contained a marriage bed of habitual boredom, transforming him, transforming her, into a sedate couple of long standing, without surprises. 'It's the thrill of the hunt,' he mocks himself, to explain away the difference. But, still, he notes the influence of otherness. The neighbourhood itself, he imagines, was zoned by someone with a map at city hall who never visited the actual streets. Three houses up, at the corner, there is a Presbyterian church with a tiny cemetery behind it. Diagonally across the intersection – and here Ken can see the compass point arcing across the map, bisecting the street – a Mr. Muffins bread factory stands behind a chain-link fence, six or eight trucks in permanent residence on several city lots' worth of concrete, lowering property values enough for Ken to be able to afford the street.

His boot heel catches on a section of sidewalk split and raised and he grabs at Tony's arm, his hand clamping just above his brother's elbow. 'Cross here,' he says.

'Shouldn't I look both ways first?' Tony asks. 'Don't be paternal with me.'

'Was I?'

'Since I was born. That's the difference between us. You were born middle-aged, and I just wanted to be old enough to take control of my own childhood.'

'Is that what you think?' Ken pushes his hands deep into the pockets of his jacket, watches his feet as he steps up onto the curb. He can feel his own smile, and turns to face the road, away from the streetlights.

'I remember exactly one time that you did anything even remotely juvenile.' Tony's voice is precise, too exact. Ken remembers taking the train home from college, having smoked until he was 'off like Jack the Bear,' and being the only passenger able to walk a straight line on the shifting floor, even on a curve. A powerful impetus, the fear of losing control.

'And that was?' he prompts.

'You were out someplace, late, and I took the top bunk. When you got home you didn't even say anything, just grabbed the bottom sheet and pulled me off, pillow, blankets and all. Dad came running in and dragged you out of the room, remember? I crawled into the lower bunk, imagining you were being whipped to within an inch of your life. And rightly so.'

'Tony, no,' Ken starts to laugh. 'I shouldn't even tell you this, revenge fantasies are important, but it wasn't like that at all. All he did was yell at me.'

'Yelling's okay, as long as he put the fear of God into you.'

'But he said, he said,' Ken stops, holding onto a No Parking sign for support. 'He said, "Your brother could have landed on his head and I don't have time to raise a brain-damaged child."'

'That's funny?' Tony steps back, the bottom of his face in shadow. Ken gasps, recovering, holds one hand out for forgiveness just as Tony's laugh barks out. 'It is, isn't it? It is funny. Oh, God.'

From the sidewalk, they can tell that Hoagy Heaven is closed but, together, they cross the empty parking lot and stand in front of the window. The only light inside is from the fluorescent tubes of the glass-fronted refrigerators.

'I guess we're out of luck.'

'Maybe it's just as well.' Tony shields his eyes with his cupped hands, peering in. 'Purple and orange vinyl all over the place, in there.'

'The hospital cafeteria is red and yellow. It might still be open, you could get something there,' Ken suggests.

'I'll get a Pecan Sandie on my way home. I'm not going to the hospital.' Tony turns away, takes a few steps, stops and leans against the window. 'I've forgotten where the bus stop is,' he says, keeping his back to Ken.

'Just past the lights,' Ken says.

'I used to know that. Funny, not to remember.'

'He might not make it, Tony.' Ken isn't sure he's said this out loud until Tony turns, his mouth open, face slack.

'You think I don't know? You don't have to tell me that. But

I'm not going to see him. I can't stand sick people. It makes my flesh crawl to think about old people, about disease. Hospitals!' He shakes his head, like a horse cut by its bit, and wipes the back of his hand across his mouth.

'But you're here. And you didn't come home for the holiday.' Ken is leaning back, has to move his feet to keep his balance.

'I came because you called me, long distance, at eight-thirty in the morning. I know the conventions. That doesn't mean I agree with the sentiment. I did my part, okay? Now I'm going home, to Dad's house. I still have my keys.' He turns and walks quickly away, about six steps, then slows to a normal pace.

Ken looks up at the sky, for the stars in the few constellations he can name, but they are obliterated by the brightness of the night-time city. Denial, he thinks, followed by anger, bargaining, depression. But that is not the order that concerns him. From another part of him, a different sequence presents itself: guilt, confession, penance followed by absolution.

'Tony!' His voice is loud on the nearly deserted street. Tony looks back from the corner, where he is waiting for the light to change although there is no apparent traffic. 'Tony, even if he dies, it doesn't mean you have to grow up.' He watches, just long enough to tell that his brother has heard, and crosses back to his own street, looking down at his boots against the sidewalk, managing to miss some, but not all, of the cracks. He stops beside the Mr. Muffins fence.

He has never smelled the bakery in the daytime, imagining the building was merely a bread factory, housing row after row of plastic-wrapped loaves stacked to the ceiling. The fragrance was obscured by car exhaust, bus fumes, the dry odour like stale talc that rose from the asphalt sidewalks. Now he stands in a warm puff of yeasty redolence and is overwhelmed by images of home: Mother taking fresh bread from the oven; running over the cool green grass, playing in the water sprinkler on a hot afternoon; the squeak of red wagon wheels as the lemonade stand is pulled to the corner bus stop, to catch the commuter trade; the slow pitching and leather slap of ball to glove during a twilight game of catch.

After an extended, longing moment, he realizes that the images in his mind are remembered from television commercials. Such things have never happened in his own life.

A Slow Dissolve

CONRAD STANDS and raises one arm when he sees Norma enter the restaurant. He recognizes her posture of hesitation: she thinks it is lady-like for a woman not to appear confident in a bar. Once he is sure she has noticed him, he walks towards her being careful, careful, not to move more than half-way across the room. Drinking makes Conrad introspective. Norma is twenty minutes late and Conrad, who was almost twenty minutes early, has filled the time at the bar. Her arrival, now, comes only moments before he would start to feel furtive, noticeably alone in a public place.

Norma disappoints him by declining a drink; he had, with some effort, maintained a second space at the bar. Instead, they are ushered to a table, led by a shepherdess with full skirts, exposed cleavage, and laced-up sandals. Conrad misses a step, rocking on his heels, so he can fall behind and see Norma from the back. He can tell her frost-grey shirtwaist is pure silk, and her hair, re-created by the studio where she has landed a television series, is strikingly, even stunningly, unnatural; that is, hair could never look so good naturally. He glances down at his own clothes – the ice-blue shirt, snowy linen slacks and jacket – and is reassured that they look like a couple. Conrad and Norma. Just like old times.

They order with rapid, familiar assurance – they'll split a Caesar; Conrad can fill up on the rolls; Norma pushes the saucer of butter pats to his side of the table – and agree on a wine after only two suggestions, a dry white, low in calories. Conrad's comment, 'If I owned a restaurant I'd call it the Wine and Wiener, and the house wine would be *Schloss Lederhosen*,' is lost as Norma tells him about her new job. Conrad watches her face. Like many attractive women, like many actresses, when she speaks the evenness of her features becomes bland: she looks somehow unfinished behind the animation of her monologue, the page of a book rather than the story.

'It's not acting, not really,' she concludes, and Conrad imagines this is an apology for her success. She's discounting the distance between them, as if this were only the result of her elevated status. He allows himself a less charitable thought: the series, which has yet to air, may be a dog; she's establishing her superiority to the material.

'Mostly,' she says, 'I just shake this hair around and get chased by strange men.' She tosses her head, illustrating the technique.

There is more light here than at the bar. The walls are lined with wrought-iron candelabra sprouting, like antlers, from Chianti bottles. Conrad feels his vision is clearer, as if the wine has neutralized the bourbon he had earlier. He feels gregarious, agreeable. Charity returns to him: of course Norma will be superior to the material; his opinion matters to her. 'Keeping in mind,' he offers around a mouthful of romaine, 'that all men are strange as hell.'

'Yes?' Norma says, the question a statement of dismissal. 'Of course, I wanted you to be the one to celebrate with me,' she goes on, using what she would be first to call her 'actressy' voice. Conrad has a matching, 'actorish' voice, resonant with authority, that may have thinned with lack of practice. He clears his throat experimentally, but remains silent.

'I was so happy, you know, I couldn't contain it. I grabbed a loaf of bread and started throwing little chunks off the balcony for the birds. It was wonderful, none of those park pigeons noticed, just the little wrens. Sparrows? The brown ones. They would stay close to the ground and all move at once, like a chorus line. Except for the star, you know, the one who got the bread. He'd fly off with it.' Norma's hands wing through the air, describing the motion.

'Yeah,' Conrad says, intending the single word to indicate both interest and understanding. Actually, his interest is less with the anecdote than the fact that just a few years earlier, as students, they might have been in the same restaurant, the kind of 'young' place where the waiters say, 'Hi, I'm Michael,' and help you choose a cheap wine. Tonight, Michael had caused a small shock of recognition in Conrad, a recognition of the time he's moved through. Although he notes the waiter has a scrubbed look, busting out with health and energy – a look Conrad can no longer achieve, not even with nine hours' sleep – he resists the idea that a few years can make that difference, can possibly matter, change people. The waiter is timeless in black slacks and white shirt, a half-apron tied around his waist like a newsboy from a different era.

'I've never owned, let alone worn, a pair of dark blue or black slacks,' Conrad says suddenly, with the fervency of a promise kept.

Norma looks up at him, her head tipped to one side.

'This isn't a suit, either,' he says, pointing at his jacket, pointing down to include his slacks, invisible to her under the table. This seems important.

'And?'

'I guess I mean there are fates I've avoided. Like having to say, "Hello, I'm Conrad and I'll be your waiter this evening. I am also an actor and a cab driver." You know?'

'No, I don't know.' Norma's fork scrapes against her plate. 'Is that supposed to be a dig?'

'Not at you,' Conrad shakes his head. 'Sorry.' Of course, Norma is really an actress now. They had planned on this, years ago, lying on either his bed or hers, and he was to be her leading man in plays of relevance and insight. Now she has a part in a television series, shaking her hair and getting chased by strange men, and Conrad, if he doesn't consider it too deeply, is content to write promotional copy for a paint and wallpaper company.

There is a long sliver of oil-slick anchovy on the side of the wooden salad bowl. He regards it with a careful appraisal. In school, finally, he had chosen to concentrate on Sociology rather than Theatre Arts, hoping to find patterns of behaviour, actions performed by a species, something larger than personal ego. That decision no longer matters; he can't change back.

Silently toasting the thought, Conrad pours the last of the wine into Norma's glass. His own glass is clouded from contact with his hand, with his mouth.

Michael is over immediately. 'More wine?'

'God, I don't think so.' Norma raises her eyebrows at Conrad. 'I think just coffee.'

'Sure?' Conrad asks.

'I'm sure.'

'Two coffee, then. And a cognac,' Conrad says to the waiter. Then, feeling a vague sense of impropriety, he adds, 'Mike.'

'Two coffee,' Michael repeats, taking the empty bottle from the table. He cradles it in one arm, reaching to the dishes on the table, then changes his mind and walks away, swinging the bottle at his side, one finger stuck into its neck.

'Anyway, did I tell you it was incredibly windy out?' Norma resumes her story, speaking around the cigarette she is trying to light. The match heads keep breaking off; one, two, three. Finally she leans over and lights her cigarette off the candle burning in a glass cylinder on the table. She takes a deep, luxurious drag and exhales with theatrical relish. 'So, I'm standing on the balcony in my dressing gown, tossing down little chunks of bread. And calling out things like – my God – "Here little birds. Don't push. Share now." Have you ever noticed how childish you get when you're alone? I thought they were getting a little out of hand, pushing each other into the road and flying across the street into the park. I didn't want the pigeons coming over, either, but I pretended I was only thinking about the sparrows.'

'They are carriers, pigeons,' Conrad agrees.

'No, they're not, not these ones. Carrier pigeons have been extinct since the radio was invented. Where have you been?'

'I meant, carriers of disease.'

'Your coffee,' Michael announces. He puts the two cups on the table, a snifter of cognac in front of Conrad, and starts to clear off the other dishes.

Conrad, as usual, has a pile of crumbs under his plate, pushed there during the course of the meal. He glances up at the waiter, saying, 'Sorry,' in an unintentionally coy voice. To cover his tone, he turns back to Norma and says, 'I'll never be smooth. Did I ever tell you I have this friend who wipes off his glass between sips? Literally sips, too, not great gulps.' A sidelong glance confirms the waiter's tolerant grin. Conrad sips his cognac, rolls it across his tongue before swallowing.

'Nick's compulsive,' Norma answers, her voice strong with the absolute authority of a well-dressed woman in a public place. She swallows the last of her wine and puts the glass on the table. Michael picks it up.

'Sure he is, but it's very smooth, don't you think?' He passes his own smudged glass to the waiter, who pulls his free hand from an apron pocket to take it. 'All done,' Conrad says, then looks up and smiles. Norma thinks being alone makes one childish.

'Compulsive, really,' Norma goes on, as if uninterrupted. 'He also rinses out those little bags that lettuce come in. Lettuces? Letti? Whatever. He uses them – the bags – to make little greenhouses for his plants.'

'Oh.'

They occupy themselves with the ritual of adding cream to their coffee. Norma never had sugar in her apartment, and Conrad has lost his taste for it. He folds the paper triangle that had contained cream into a tight square before wedging it under his saucer. He wonders how Norma is privy to the details of Nick's life. He won't ask; Nick is a common friend, he can leave it at that. But – how has he not noticed this? – it's been months since he last saw the man. He tries to recall their last meeting, anything said or done that might have been final. Nothing comes to mind, except the familiar thought that this condition is no longer unusual. There was a time when men went west, as pioneers, never to be heard from again. There was a time when men went to foreign lands, as soldiers, and returned as heroes, or victims, or remained, forever, memories. There was a time when a man's absence was explained by those events, by nothing less than the larger issues of migration, or patriotism. Conrad has been taught that this changed with the affluence following the Second World War; homecomings were changed to reunions; community lives became parallel lines; the affordable automobile had only to be put into gear to turn an old life into history. Cars and cash, he thinks, symptom and result of mobility, casual contact. When he lifts his coffee to his mouth, his face feels flushed with the rising steam. He presses the sleeve of his jacket against his cheek.

'The birds?' he prompts.

'Right. Where was I? Yes, they were flying across the road, very low, when they got a piece of bread. And I'm calling, "Be careful, little birdies." Would you believe it? No sooner have I called out – and I'm on the balcony in my robe, remember – "Careful!" than, my God, a car comes out of nowhere and hits the bird that's carrying the biggest piece of bread.

'I could have died. Oh, wow, how do I tell you this?

'The first thing I did was squint down to see if it had been killed. Like, try to get a good look at a sparrow on concrete from thirty feet or whatever. But I thought I saw it move. I did see it move, it waved a wing at me, so I went inside and called the Humane Society.'

Conrad pushes his hair back from his forehead, his fingers bluntly probing for the coarser, grey stands. He discovered the first of these, a single grey hair, one morning in Norma's bathroom.

'Jesus, would you look at this?' he asked her, stepping into the living-room, holding his hair back, flat against his temple. 'It makes me feel like the picture of Dorian Gray.'

'Dorian Gray, you?' Norma shook her head. 'I don't think so. You're about the most benign person I know. Morally, I mean.'

'No, not Dorian Gray. The picture. I'm being sacrificed for someone else's sins. Out there, somewhere,' he waved at the glass balcony doors to indicate the city beyond. 'Someone is living it up at my expense. You'll have to hide me in the closet as this gets too obvious, as I shrivel and rot with corruption.' He raised one shoulder into a hump and lurched across the room towards her, making a deep, growling noise low in his throat, dragging one foot. 'Who could it be?'

'Stop it,' Norma said, backing away from him. 'This isn't funny.'

'Who? Who?' Conrad croaked, twisting one hand into a palsied claw, reaching out to touch her face, having backed her into a corner.

'All right,' Norma yelled, slapping one palm into his chest, hard. 'It's me. It's me, okay? God, you're such a fool sometimes.'

'You?' Conrad stood in the middle of the room, baffled, feeling something slip out of his control, a dull, bruised feeling to match the numb spot on his rib cage where Norma had bruised the skin over his heart, knocked the air from his lungs.

'Why the Humane Society?' he asks.

'What was I supposed to do if it wasn't dead? Go down and wring its neck? In my dressing gown? I figured they'd be able to do something. The phone cord reaches the balcony, you know that, so I was able to stand out there and look at this bird, and they tell me it'll take two hours to get a truck over. A truck, for God's sake. Two hours. While I'm standing there, though, and this is the part that really rips me up, another car comes tootling down the road and runs the damn thing over. It was obviously very dead then, so I told the Humane Society to forget it.' Norma puts her arms out flat on the table and bends her head forward, over her coffee cup.

Conrad sips at his coffee, then takes a mouthful of cognac, watching her, knowing the gesture indicates a dramatic pause. Norma acts for television, with its quick cuts and freeze frames. As audience, he may not be expected to do anything other than sit here.

Noticing her cup is empty, wanting a distraction, he leans back to get the waiter's attention. Michael is across the room, opening a bottle of wine for another couple. Conrad catches his eye just as the cork comes out of the bottle with an audible pop. Michael looks at him blankly for a moment, then smiles and nods. Conrad lights a cigarette and stares at the other couple, younger and somehow more intense than he and Norma must appear. The woman leans forward, whispering something; the man, smiling, takes the bottle from Michael and fills her glass.

Turning back to Norma, who is sitting up now, watching him watch the others, Conrad asks, 'So what did you do then?'

'Do? What could I do? I went back into the living room, sat down and cackled like an idiot for twenty minutes. I mean, I just hated myself for reacting like that, but what else could I do? I finally had to take a couple Valium to get myself under control.'

'I hope they didn't keep you up,' Conrad says, pleased they have this old joke between them. One night when he was at her place he'd had a hard time falling asleep. Not wanting to disturb her although he felt, perversely, that she was to blame for his insomnia, he had taken one of the pills – a small, blue tablet – from the top of her dresser. The pill turned out to be a diuretic from an old prescription of hers and he had spent the rest of the night going to the bathroom. It seems a very long time ago, now, that innocent error.

'Yes?' Michael leans over Conrad's shoulder. 'More coffee?' Turning awkwardly to Norma, his balance shifts and he presses against Conrad, recovering.

'Please,' Norma says, suddenly prim. 'I think I need another.'

'Two,' Conrad confirms, addressing the waiter directly.

'Sure thing,' Michael says. He stops to retie his apron before taking the cups from the table. The paper triangle drops from the bottom of Conrad's saucer and lies on the table, slowly unfolding like something newborn. In a swift move, Michael picks this up and pockets it. Conrad twists his neck to watch him cross to the coffee station. When Michael gets there, he turns back and smiles, the same quick smile he had offered from across the room earlier.

Conrad also smiles, with a slight nod of his head. It is a friendly, impulsive gesture, an acknowledgement.

'Well, he's all over you,' Norma says, archly. 'But that's no reason to embarrass me in public.'

'For God's sake,' Conrad responds, annoyed at himself. The time between then and now dissolves in this moment. 'Get off my back.'

'I'll bet that's not what you told Seth,' Norma counters, hissing. 'You just couldn't wait for him to get on your back,' she adds, viciously.

'Don't be ridiculous. What was I supposed to think of him, the way you two were always crawling over each other?' This is true. Conrad had thought he was being replaced by Seth in Norma's life. An anger, a misunderstood jealousy, had filled him and, when Norma told him Seth wanted to meet him for a drink, Conrad had imagined a man-to-man encounter, a masculine settling of accounts, possibly a fist-fight.

If he had been less preoccupied with what one did with one's thumb when making a fist, he thinks now, he would have been able to see that the evening had been set up as a date. Seth was to pick him up at Norma's, since he had a car and could drive the two of them, Conrad and Seth, to a bar that was comfortable and quiet enough for conversation. *Dinkies*, no less, the name of the bar.

Norma was lying on the couch, reading, when Seth arrived. Conrad was in the bedroom, having decided moments before to change into boots and a corduroy jacket over jeans. He knotted a tie over a sports shirt. Stylish but rugged; a good compromise.

In the living room he shook hands with Seth, who was wearing a tweed jacket over a turtleneck sweater that disappeared under his beard. He bent to kiss Norma goodbye, a gesture more for Seth's sake than Norma's.

'I don't think we'll be late,' he said, throwing responsibility for this to Seth with a questioning look.

'I'll get him home early, m'am,' Seth said, and Norma laughed, confusing Conrad.

'Be good,' Norma said.

And they were. Seth had told amusing stories about married people, about couples, including his own parents, although the punchlines to these were rather pointed, in a bitchy, patronizing way. Conrad felt he should apologize for his own dullness, felt that he was contributing nothing to the conversation. He wanted to do something for Seth, to show that he was having a good time, how relieved he was that this encounter was not going to end anywhere near a fist-fight.

Conrad got back to Norma's just after three in the morning. He was irritated to find her still up, still reading. He had wanted to spend the rest of the night with Seth; dressing again and leaving the way he had done made him feel sticky and unclean. He had felt obligated to return, and that increased his annoyance.

'Did you have a nice time?' Norma asked, watching him as he undressed, dropping his clothes to the floor as he crossed to the bathroom.

'Very,' Conrad answered, stepping into the bathtub and pulling the shower curtain closed.

'So, where did you go?' Norma shouted over the sound of running water, obviously just on the other side of the shower curtain.

'We went back to his place.'

'What for?'

'I can't hear you.'

Norma pulled the shower curtain back, ignoring the water that sprayed out into the bathroom. 'Did he tell you he was a fag?' Her voice was hard, triumphant, as though she had just played some final, wild card in a high-stakes game.

'In a manner of speaking, yes,' Conrad replied, calmly. 'Please let go of the curtain. There's a draft.'

'You bastard!'

This was the last Conrad heard, concentrating his attention on his own body, its hollows and planes.

After a long time he got out of the shower, dried himself slowly and, wearing a towel draped around his waist – suddenly not wanting Norma to see him naked – he walked into the bedroom. Her body on the bed, despite his familiarity with it, seemed foreign, demanding. He thought of Seth's duplication of his own lines, easily understood satisfactions.

'Do you want me to stay?' he asked, accepting her right to him, a right based on the time they spent together, a claim no less important than that of family members; the obligations of a shared past.

'No,' she said, stubbing out her cigarette into the ashtray on the night table. 'Yes,' she said, reaching for the package and taking out another cigarette. The angles of her face, her superb bone structure, were burnished in the glow of a match. 'I don't know. Do you want to?'

The towel dropped from Conrad's body as he moved into the room, one hand brushing against her breast as he reached across her for a cigarette.

Later that year he got a job with the paint and wallpaper company. He saw Seth sometimes, on Seth's terms always: he saw Norma less and less. Then Seth moved to the Coast. Conrad resigned himself to his own life: he thought that would be enough.

'Can we talk about something else?' Norma asks. 'I didn't go out and get this dress so we could sit here and talk about Seth.'

'You brought it up,' Conrad shrugs, agreeable enough not to point out that she also set it up, his involvement with the other man. 'So, what now?' he asks, knowing the scene in the restaurant is ending.

'Would you like to come back to my place for a drink? I have a bottle of vermouth, that good kind you like.' Norma shreds her cream triangle, a flutter of hands with improbably long nails, and piles the torn bits in the ashtray. Conrad has to push them aside to butt his cigarette. 'There's a good late movie on television,' she adds. 'One of the classics.'

'That might be nice,' he says, with what he hopes is a proper detachment. He'll keep himself open.

'Of course,' Norma qualifies. 'Some people are coming over early. You understand.'

Michael comes over with their coffee, carefully placing the cups on the table.

'What, now?' Conrad asks, having forgotten they were waiting for these. The evening seems too close to its end for more of anything. 'Okay, okay,' he adds, to no one, his voice a low murmur.

Michael holds an inverted, empty ashtray over the full one on the table, lifts both away, then returns the empty one, righted.

'Will that be all?' He asks the question directly to Conrad. His hands are folded in front of him, over the ashtray.

'Yes, thanks. Just the check,' Conrad says. After the waiter leaves he adds, to Norma, 'People coming over? I understand.' He comes down very hard on the last word, to suggest the all-encompassing nature of his understanding, to, in effect, efface the people she has coming over.

'Think about it. Now, excuse me. I'll be right back.'

Conrad watches her cross the room, watches the faces that turn to look at her. She'd spoken easily, but she hadn't sounded insincere. An actress. He wonders about her story, doubting her only purpose was to entertain him. Somehow, he thinks, the story is about, if not them, at least him. Whatever meaning she had intended escapes him, yet even this feeling of loss, of not knowing, is not new to him. He thinks of the endings of television movies, when stills from the movie just ended are run behind the closing credits. Once he had thought the effect was to create distance, a kind of debriefing before the next programme started. Now he wonders if the stills might not be planned to create recognition. As audience, he would feel his experience was a valid one. Yes, he would think, watching again, that's really how it happened, that's how it happened to me. Familiarity can be manipulated.

Michael arrives with the check on a plastic salver. Preoccupied, Conrad reaches over and, in the movement, his hand is over the waiter's. On impulse, Conrad closes his fingers. Michael makes no move to pull back.

Conrad releases the hand, reaches for his wallet, and pulls out two large bills. He glances at the check, the dim purple figures meaningless to him, then shifts his focus to Norma, making her way back to the table. Roughly, as though running out of time, he shoves the bills into Michael's hands.

'Take this.'

Michael looks down at the bills in his hands, then back to Conrad's face. He nods, with a quick, understanding smile. It is not necessary for Conrad to add, 'Keep the change.'

Norma takes a step back, with an exaggerated courtesy, to let the waiter pass her. Conrad keeps his head down, looking at the rainbow of slick oils on the surface of his coffee.

'Well?' she asks.

'We can get a cab,' he says.

Outside, the evening has the coolness of early spring, and Conrad is sobered and thoughtful. He can see a cab coming down the street, its top light dim as a distant star, and he raises his arm, waving. Norma puts her arm through his when he returns it to his side. He lets her leave her hand on the inside of his elbow, but moves his feet further apart, to maintain his own balance.

'Nice,' she says.

'It was,' Conrad agrees, because he owes it to her. He doesn't voice his hesitancy that the evening has eluded him. 'I don't go out much anymore.'

'No, this,' she shakes his arm gently. 'We were good together.'

'Back then.' Conrad steps back so her arm slides against his hip before it drops to her side. 'Here we go,' he adds, for the taxi has drawn up to the curb beside them. He opens the back door and holds his hand out for her to balance herself, getting in. He names her address to the cabbie, including her apartment number. Then he straightens and slaps wildly at his hip pocket.

'Damn,' he says, leaning down slightly to face her in the back seat, his own body safely outside the car. 'I left my credit card in there. I'll have to go back. You go ahead.' He slams the door quickly, the thud ricocheting off the walls of the buildings around them and cutting off whatever she has said, her lips moving silently behind the window. He turns away, keeping his back to her until he hears the car start up and move away.

He remains on the sidewalk after she is gone. His own quick lie amazes him. He had not planned on that, not even when he first suggested a taxi. His own car, in fact, is in a public lot behind the restaurant, and it costs him three dollars and seventy-five cents to cover the time it has sat there.

Victims of Gravity

ON HIS FIRST SUNDAY as a married man, Nick wakes slowly. 'It's as if they were never pierced at all,' the woman had said, stroking her earlobe. 'I just stopped wearing the earrings.' They were on a subway, rattling through blocks of light and dark. Nick had struggled to see her face, but she turned away from him, exposing only the line of her neck. While his dream shreds and recedes to its soft world of symbols and solutions he lets himself drift into consciousness.

With his eyes still closed, he takes inventory; his arms here, legs there, his head sunk deep in the pillow. He can feel the cat sleeping against his side, solid as a ham. 'I'm okay,' he tells himself. 'I'm going to be okay,' he amends.

'Good morning,' he calls out, hearing Linda in the kitchen, the sound of running water. This sound is so mundane, so clear with everyday purpose, he feels it must be a response to his own resolution; he is going to be okay. He flips himself out of bed, sending the cat from the room at a fast trot, landing squarely on his feet.

Over breakfast, Nick decides to re-enter his life slowly, taking one thing at a time.

'I'm going up to the school, for softball,' he tells Linda. 'Want to come and root for me?'

'You must be joking. I don't have time for anything like that. There are a million things for me to do before we go to my folks'.' She is wearing an old pair of corduroy slacks, worn bald at the seat and inside the thighs, with one of Nick's shirts half-buttoned over these. Nick thinks she looks boyish and sloppy, and absolutely charming.

'That's tonight?' Nick asks, remembering the invitation, but vaguely, as if it had been given to someone else; someone else must have responded. 'We just saw them last week.' He carries his plate to the sink and stands there, looking out the window.

'Couldn't we make it some other time?'

'Listen, when you get back,' Linda says, 'could you leave your shoes outside? I want to do something with these floors.'

'My shoes?' Nick steps back from the sink and looks down at his Nikes. Under them, the floor looks as it always has, small grey and blue squares spreading out in concentric circles, orbiting farther and farther away from him. He realizes he's holding his breath and exhales carefully, so he won't sigh. He is being cautious and formal, a married person.

The cat crosses in front of him, weightless with feline purpose. 'The cat comes in on little fog feet,' Nick says, thinking Eric would have liked that. Nick likes it; it feels like his first appropriate response to his environment in weeks.

'What?' Linda's eyes are opaque.

'Never mind.' Nick turns his back. 'You're sure you don't want to come with me?'

'I'm sure.' Linda comes up beside him, nudging him out of the way so she can reach the tap to rinse out her coffee mug. 'You have fun.'

By the time Nick finishes getting ready, Linda is on the phone, confirming the time for dinner with her mother. Nick remembers his own mother, sitting in the kitchen to talk on the black, wall-mounted telephone. She wore, always, a two-piece wool suit; her legs – one almost completely coiled around the other when she was perched on the edge of the chrome dinette chair – were encased in shiny nylon stockings of an orange sheen he has not seen since. On a Sunday, the table in front of her would support her hat and gloves. He waves as he passes the kitchen, his hand raised to his temple like a salute, then stops when he hears her call out to him.

'Yes?' He stands still. The doorknob is smooth and egg-shaped in his hand.

'You won't forget, about your shoes?'

'I won't forget.' Nick lets the door close behind him and steps into the clear morning, the sounds of the city coming to him all at once, as if they had been waiting for his appearance. He walks down Century, on the sunny side of the street, to the corner of Elm, before crossing to the school campus.

ON SUNDAYS, before, Nick played softball with Eric on the back campus of the high school where they both taught. Some of the seniors joined them, enough to make two short teams. Eric, who handled his history classes with a firm authority, was subjected to extensive razzing about his pitching, which was slow and loose.

'Drill it man, burn it home,' the guys yelled at him. 'Don't make it so easy.'

Eric laughed out loud and pitched the way he always did, in a predictable straight line over the plate. Then, turning to watch the struck ball, he had an amazed expression, as if no one had ever connected with one of his pitches before. In Special Ed. class at college, when they were learning American Sign Language, nobody had to look at Eric's hands to figure out what he was trying to say. Everything was written on his face.

'It wasn't so easy,' he said, sheepish, when Nick and he and his girl-friend Peg went for pizza and beer. 'It had a little dance to it.'

'Dance, hell. It was a funeral. Hey, what's a good dance for a funeral, Peg?' Nick wanted to include her in the conversation, or to have her feel included. He wasn't sure what level of familiarity was expected of him. His first year at the school, Peg was on maternity leave, so he knows more about her than he's heard from her, more than he's heard, even, from Eric. He knows she's a year older than he, that she was a professional dancer, jazz or modern, for a few years before marrying and taking the job in the school office, and that she had a baby boy. Mark? Matthew? Michael? No, Matthew is right. 'A gavotte?'

'Too formal,' Peg shook her head, brushing a few crumbs from her cheek. 'A Tarantella, the way you guys play, all formless and frenzied until you drop.'

'Tarantella. Tarantula,' Eric said, splaying the fingers of one hand rigidly on the tabletop, pushing them down from the wrist, then lifting up. 'Push-ups on a mirror.'

'No, that's this one.' Peg put the fingers of both hands together, flexing them against each other. 'I should know. It's about Matt's level.'

'How is Matt?' Nick asked. Once, when he was playing outfield, he glanced over the campus to his left and saw her, Peg, sitting on the hood of Eric's car, combing her hair in the morning light, before the sun was directly overhead. That, along with the sophistication he imagined because she was divorced with a four-year-old son, warmed him with an easy, transparent want.

'He's great.' Peg raised one hand and deliberately brought it, fisted, into the space between her breasts. 'My heart is full,' she said solemnly, without a trace of self-consciousness. Eric snorted and Nick was saved from embarrassment by recognizing the line from a movie.

'Saint Peg,' Eric intoned, causing Nick to choke on his beer. 'Saint Peg the Miracle-less.'

'Oh, stop it,' Peg said, and Eric assumed a posture of contrition, lowering his head and feigning great fascination with the menu before him. 'How's, Linda?' she asked Nick, barely pausing before the name.

'Fine, I guess.' Nick heard the hesitation in her question, before the name. He wished, for a moment, he could confide in her something true and revealing, or at least make the kind of comment that a woman would find interesting. Say, 'She finds working on her doctorate is teaching her a lot about herself,' or, 'She's decided social work is an option before she locks herself into any choices.' He really doesn't know what those comments would mean. 'She doesn't go out much,' he says. 'I don't know.'

'Yes.' Peg nodded, as if she understood this.

'This place used to have lentil burgers,' Eric looked up, a lock of hair diagonally over his forehead giving him a surprised appearance. 'I don't see them here.'

'I guess no one returned them,' Peg offered.

'What?'

'The burgers, I guess no one returned them,' Peg started. Then, 'Lentil! You said, Lentil. I thought you said, Rental burgers.'

'Me, too,' Nick agreed. 'I was trying to figure out how it worked, but I couldn't get my mind any farther than that they'd come with a paper tablecloth.'

'You're both mad.' Eric sat back, crossing his arms in his shiny green bowling jacket, an authentic relic discovered at the Crippled Civilians, with 'Fraser' heavily cross-stitched over the left shoulder.

Nick reached out and pulled some melted cheese from the plate of pizza, perfectly content.

'Come on, Eric. Give me some help with this.'

THAT FRIDAY Eric was killed when his car spun out of control over a patch of road being resurfaced on the outskirts of town. The accident was not connected to events in the lives of Eric and Nick. It was pointless, fatal. Nick was twenty-eight years old; disturbing doubts about God were in his past and in his future. He was convinced, only, of his own solitude.

When Linda suggested he should not be alone after the funeral, Nick agreed. He agreed to everything; choice was not in him. He had, in fact, no concept of what his agreement would entail. Time had ceased to be continuous to him. Anything might happen. Certainly he would still be alone, with his past amputated from him he was singular and incomplete.

Less than five weeks later, with no sense of cause-and-effect, he found himself walking through a formal church wedding. There were sixty-eight guests at the reception afterwards, mostly Linda's family and their friends, all strangers to Nick. He couldn't tell you now if it had rained that day, or was sunny and clear. Later, in the photographs, he will notice that he has the first two fingers of his right hand held oblique across the palm of his left. The Sign for What. *What?*

'HEY, MR. THORNTON,' one of the guys calls to Nick as he lets himself through the chain link fence. 'Long time no see.'

'Yeah, I'm back.' Nick recognizes the boy, Bob Markham, from his class. He can't remember seeing him standing before, although he knows he's played softball almost weekly. 'What team am I on?' He stands behind the plate and picks up one of the bats, swinging it experimentally, with an exaggerated, critical concentration.

'We sort of had the teams already set up,' Bob says, looking down at the ground.

'Time stands still for no man, is that it?' Nick says. He makes a noise, a meaningless snort or chuckle, trying to reassure the boy that this distance isn't necessary, but this is artificial and painful to Nick.

'Well,' Bob looks at him, eyes slightly narrowed. 'You could be in the field.'

'Sure.' Nick nods. Then he looks, closely, at the boy in front of him. There is a patch, just where Bob's cheek angles down to his jaw, that has been missed in the last shave. The fine hairs there, too soft to be called stubble, grow all in one direction, as ordered and distinct as the petals of a flower. They are separated by no more than ten or eleven years, Nick thinks, and he takes a step forward. 'What are you planning to do after school?' he asks.

'On Sunday? Oh, I see. Well, college.'

'No, after that, even.'

'I don't know.' Bob looks uncomfortable. 'Like, get a job or something. You know, reality.'

'Reality,' Nick repeats. The word is hard-edged in his mouth, like a cracked cough drop. He waves one hand in the air in front of him, unable to articulate a question, the dismissive gesture the same as the one he uses in class when the period ends. 'Don't mind me.'

'I don't, Mr. Thornton,' Bob says. 'You know, we're all real sorry about your friend. Mr. Heinz, he was okay.' Bob stands in front of Nick as if he's about to say more, then he shrugs and puts his hands into his pockets as if they were too heavy for his arms to support.

'Yeah,' Nick agrees. 'He was okay.' He turns and starts towards the outfield. At the back of the campus he raises his arm and shouts, 'Let's get this show on the road.' Then he sees Eric at the side of the campus – knowing in the same moment it's Peg, wearing Eric's bowling jacket – and he yells, 'Hey! Hey!'

By the second 'hey' he is walking quickly towards her. She stands on the sidewalk on the other side of the fence, not watching his approach, and Nick is afraid she will bolt, start running away from him. Comic-book heroes fill his mind as he considers ways to stop her: a long, flexible arm like Elastic Man; a speed-of-light sprint like the Flash; an entangling web shot from his wrist like Spiderman. Lacking these resources, he feels clumsy and inadequate. This is similar to the feeling he had as a child, when he would wake from a dream of flight and find himself, still, a victim of gravity.

'Peg.' Nick puts one hand up, his fingers curled through the fence, and leans towards her, imprisoned behind the diamonds of wire mesh. 'I'm glad I saw you. What are you doing here?'

'I'm in the neighbourhood, Sundays,' she says, keeping her profile to him. 'Matt's reading group is just up there. I hang around.'

'Yeah? I haven't seen you.' This sounds like an accusation. 'I haven't been here, myself.' They begin walking together, Peg on the sidewalk and Nick on grass splotched with white lime powder, with the fence between them.

'Matt reads?' Nick asks, after a silence. He's imagined the reading group to be a kind of Great Books Society, intent in a discussion of *Pat the Bunny*.

'No, he's read to,' Peg says. 'Sometimes I forget he's a kid, you know? He's a friend.'

Nick pauses, searching. Then, 'What do you tell a friend, about what happened?'

'I never lied to him about life ending badly. I used to tell him he wouldn't have to worry for a long, long time. I thought his interest was personal. I never thought of anything like this.' She brushes a strand of hair from her mouth, where a light breeze has lifted it. 'I guess he won't believe me any more. Maybe he'll never ask me what makes the sky blue, and I've already done my homework on that one. You're supposed to work at having them trust you, kids. All the time.'

They come to the end of the fence, where the gate is, and Nick lets himself through to stand with her on the sidewalk.

'What now?' he asks.

They start walking up Elm, stopping together at the curb for a moment, although there's no light. They step into the street again at the same moment, as if they've been signalled to do this.

'Does Matt trust you?' Nick starts, after Peg has been quiet, walking with her head down, her hands in the pockets of the green jacket.

'I guess he does. I'm not sure what the point is. I trusted his father – like, I felt I was supposed to – and I might have been better off not to, right from the beginning. Or maybe I shouldn't have thought it was so important. You know, lower my expectations. Not make demands. Never nag.' She laughs, a short, unamused sound. 'I've said those things before, can't you tell?'

Nick scuffs the suede toe of his Nike along the sidewalk, instead of answering. Peg stops, looking down at the shoe, then points, 'Your lace.'

He kneels in front of her to re-tie his track shoe, feeling a smooth mastery of the situation as he twists the lace into a perfect bow, taking time to make the ends even. 'There.' He stands up.

'You do that just like Matt. All rigid concentration and perfection. I wonder what it means, about his personality? How's yours, are you a well-adjusted person?'

'No,' Nick says, being honest after some deliberation. 'No, I don't think that I am.'

'Sorry.' Peg looks down at her own feet, lining up the ends of her shoes with a crack in the sidewalk. 'I shouldn't have asked.'

'I didn't have to answer. I wanted to.'

'Don't do that,' Peg says, her voice sharp.

'Do what?'

'Act like there's something between us. We don't have any-thing more in common than we did six weeks ago. We don't even really know each other, okay?'

'No.' Nick leaves the single syllable uninflected.

'You know what's supposed to happen now, don't you? I'm supposed to take this off.' Peg runs one hand over the bowling jacket, under the gold collar where it meets the green body. 'And tell you that Eric would have wanted you to have it. Maybe he would have, but I'm not giving it to you. I love having this jacket all to myself. I'm even living in his apartment, did you know that? It was just about the only thing his family wasn't crazy to con-sider an asset.' She looks up at Nick, her hair wild and careless over her face. She beats at it, to push it back with a blunt, closed fist. Nick steps forward automatically, raising his hand to stop her. 'No,' she says, leaning away from him. 'I'm not going to cry. I'm being,' she stops to rub her nose with the sleeve of the jacket, 'brave. I don't have anything to share with you.'

'I guess not,' Nick agrees.

'I have to pick up my kid. Don't come with me, okay?' She turns, walking away quickly, bent over. Nick has not asked her where Eric was going to, or coming from, that night; he under-stands that he is never to know. The past is closed off. He stands on the sidewalk, imagining he can hear the softball game still in progress, way back there, going on without him.

'THE HONEYMOON COUPLE!'

He hears Ian Grant's voice boom through the door. The sound seems to displace the air in the long hall before the door is pulled open and his father-in-law stands in front of Nick and Linda.

'Well,' Ian says. 'Well, well.'

'Three holes in the ground?' Nick offers, at the same time extending his hand for a hearty pumping.

'Hi, Daddy.' Linda steps past Nick and into the living room.

She raises her arms, hands lightly closed and limp at the wrists, presenting herself for a hug.

'Hi, Lindy.'

'Is that them?' Betsy Grant's voice pierces the wall between the living room and the kitchen. 'I'll be right in.'

'Go give your mother a hug,' Ian says, pushing Linda away. 'We'll be out here. Come on, Nick.'

Nick follows the older man across the room, idly wiping his palm on the pocket flap of his jacket. He notes the difference between this room and his own living room. Here, the carpet is thick and plush, the furniture heavily upholstered. Nick lives with bare floors and pine knock-downs from a Scandinavian shop.

'Now, what can I get you to drink?'

'Scotch, I guess,' Nick says, moving closer to the liquor cabinet. Linda and her mother come out of the kitchen, close and talking quietly.

'Oh, that's good for us,' Betsy says, raising her voice. She comes up to Nick and lays one hand on his arm. 'We're having veal,' she tells him, imparting this message as a confidence.

'You know,' Nick carries a drink, diluted to the colour of winter sunlight, across the room to Linda. 'I used to think that veal came from a separate animal. Like chicken from chickens, lamb from lambs.'

'Ham from pigs, beef from cows.' Linda shakes her head. 'It doesn't hold up, that thinking.'

'Well, wait, it gets worse.' Nick picks up his glass and takes half the scotch in one swallow. 'When someone told me it comes from calves, I thought they meant these.' He almost tips the remains of his drink as he taps the muscle below the back of his knee. 'I had only learned how to spell it – calves – and I was baffled by the connection.' He looks around the room, at Betsy nursing her own drink, Ian staring past him to some other reality outside the window, Linda twisting a strand of hair around her fingers. After a silence, Nick asks, 'Am I talking funny or something? I didn't expect a big laugh, but –'

'It's a nice story,' Betsy interrupts. 'We can take our drinks to the table.'

Nick sits at his place, across the table from Linda, and eats in silence while she talks to her family about how much work she's doing to turn Nick's apartment into a 'home.'

'Really, Mummy, he keeps his socks and underwear in a toy box. Like that.'

'Oh, men,' Betsy agrees, shaking her head.

Nick imagines if he looks up Ian will give him a conspiratorial wink. He feels his temples pounding and closes his eyes, leaning forward. He opens his eyes and looks down in his lap. The white napkin there suddenly blossoms with a red, red rose. He stares, perplexed, until another spot spreads itself over the soft cloth.

'Oh, my God,' he pushes his chair back from the table. 'My nose is bleeding. Excuse me.' He leaves the room with the napkin pressed against the bridge of his nose, trying to remember what he learned about this condition in Boy Scouts: how much pressure is therapeutic? He hears the table fall silent behind him, just for a moment, then all three voices speak at once.

IN THE BATHROOM, Nick soaks the napkin and holds it against his nose, splashing cold water on his face with his other hand. After what seems a very long time the bleeding slows, then stops, the water running down the drain tinged with pink, then clear.

He wrings the napkin nearly dry, pats his face with it, then spreads it over the edge of the sink. With a heavy sigh, he lowers the toilet seat cover and sits down, stretching his legs out in front of him, his boots pressed against the side of the bathtub.

There is a short, soft knock on the door.

'Nick?' Linda asks, pushing the door open and stepping into the room. 'You okay?' She leans back against the door, pushing it closed.

'I guess.' Nick glances sideways at her, but remains seated. 'I'm not making a very good impression.'

'I told them it was probably the scotch.'

'Oh, great. Thanks a lot. Now they think I can't handle liquor.'

'No, it's not like that at all. What's the matter with you?'

'You know what I heard in the staff lounge? Remember that television show, *Wild Kingdom*, where they'd go after a different animal each week? One of the teachers was saying that the whole thing was a fake. Like when the narrator would say,' Nick lowers his voice, aiming for a broadcasting tone, '"On our way to observe the mating dance of the snowy egret, we spotted this fellow in a bit of a jam." And there'd be a woolly marmot or something – a furry little mammal, always – stuck in a tree. The crew would stop and rescue it with all this equipment they had with them. "After giving the little fellow a helping hand, we were back on the egret trail."

'Do you remember that?'

'I remember those shows. So what?' Linda turns to stand in front of the sink, the counter at the level where her blouse tucks into her skirt, avoiding the damp napkin.

'Brian, this other teacher, was saying that they were all faked. That woolly marmot was put in the tree by the crew in the first place. Even the egrets were from the San Diego Zoo or someplace.' Nick shakes his head slowly. 'It was all a big fake.'

'Is there a point to this?' Linda leans forward, closer to her reflection. She combs her fingers through her hair, flipping the ends over her shoulders. Then she rubs at one corner of her mouth with her ring finger, frowning. She props one hip against the sink and turns back to Nick. 'What are you trying to tell me?'

'Don't you feel betrayed by that? Like, there's absolutely nothing left to count on in the world. I'd always reassured myself that no matter what happened to us,' he waves his hand in a sweeping arc to include all of humanity, 'in all the aridity and disenchantment,' now he raises his hand, loosely fisted, 'the wild kingdom was still unfolding according to plan. It was still a beautiful world.' He falls silent, rubbing one hand back and forth over the toilet paper holder. The unrolled paper jerks up and down like an elevator trying to level itself.

'Wait.' Linda crosses her arms over her chest. 'I want to be sure I understand this. You are upset, to the point of a nosebleed, because *Wild Kingdom* was faked. Maybe faked. Have I got that right? Is there anything else?'

Nick brushes at the knees of his slacks, then leans forward, putting his elbows on his thighs and cupping his chin in his hands. How can he tell her he needs her to sit on the hood of his car, combing her hair in the clear light of morning while he plays games to win her, again and again? How can he tell her that the game is what he is playing for, rather than the outcome? How can he tell her the condition of his kitchen floor gives him no clues to the inevitability of his own survival?

'I think,' he says slowly. 'This isn't going to work out. Us.'

'What? What are you talking about?' Linda pulls back from the sink, standing unsupported in the middle of the bathroom. 'I'm willing to work at this relationship.'

'Relationship? Well, yes, sure.' He lets his voice trail off, unable to say anything for a while. 'You're right. We could work at this, the relationship, and sort of polite each other to death, staying together. But that's not what I want.' He looks up at her.

'Go ahead, then. Tell me,' Linda commands, raising her hands to her neck, closing her fingers into knots against the soft skin there.

'No.' Nick shakes his head. He curls his toes inside his boots, to take up less space, a fetal position of the feet. His insteps press against leather, the smooth hide of some animal.

'You started this.'

'Okay.' Nick takes a breath and fixes his gaze into the middle distance. 'This is not going to work and I want out.'

'Don't say that.' Linda lowers her voice as she speaks. 'I can't believe you said that to me in a bathroom. Why did you marry me at all?'

'You didn't want me to be alone.' Nick shrugs, to discount the cost of admitting this; it's vaguely impolite, self-serving, to remind one of a favour performed.

'Alone? Alone? What about me?'

'You've got them,' Nick tips his head at the bathroom door.

'Don't you say a word to them. Leave them out of this. We are going back out there and you are not going to say anything about this. I'm not discussing this in here.'

Nick stands and turns, bending to lift the toilet seat. 'I'll be out in a bit.' He pulls down his fly. 'Do you mind?'

'Remember,' Linda cautions, letting herself out of the room and pulling the door closed after her.

WHEN SHE'S GONE, Nick does up his fly, puts the cover back down on the toilet and sits with his body twisted at the waist so he can rest his forehead on the cool sink. His life, to this moment, arranges itself behind him. In front of him, the marbled counter is blurred and indistinct. He is too close to focus properly.

When his mother died, he had been judged too young to attend the burial; he was allowed in the church, but not to the grave. One of his mother's friends had taken him to her car, where she had tilted the rear-view mirror so she could reapply her lipstick, talking to him all the while around that pink cylinder. Later, they went to a restaurant ('I know you boys are always hungry,' she said) and this woman, nameless to him, chain-smoked. Nick's mother never smoked in public; this woman never stopped. Hearing the word 'funeral' when it spread through the teachers' lounge, Nick had not thought of his friend, not thought of Eric at all. His mind had been filled with this woman, exhaling smoke through her nose while biting into a toasted club sandwich.

HE RAISES his head and looks around, as if he expects to see that someone has come in and joined him. He stands quietly and goes over to the door, turning the knob slowly and pulling it open silently. He steps into the hall, listening intently, then walks down the hall away from the living room.

The master bedroom door is open, and Nick steps into the room walking on tiptoe, with an unnecessary stealth. He can hear Linda and her parents laughing, the clink of glass and a scraping sound, a knife against china.

There is, as Nick had hoped there would be, a telephone in the darkened room, on the night table at the right side of the queen-sized bed. Nick remains standing, rather than creasing the bedspread, and picks up the receiver, holding it to his ear until he hears the dial tone. Then, pleased to be able to do this by memory, he dials Eric's number. Before the first ring, during the confused jangle of far-off, electronic noises, he tips his head towards the door, satisfied he can still hear Linda talking to her parents.

'Hello?' The voice that answers, on the fourth ring, is still young enough to inflect those two syllables with hope.

'Hello, Matt?' Nick speaks quickly, his voice just barely above a whisper. 'Is your mother home?'

'Mom!' Matt has obviously turned from the phone without covering the mouthpiece, calling to his mother. Nick crouches down with the effort of listening through the distance that separates them. 'Mom, it's for you. A man with a deep voice.'

With the first two fingers of his right hand, Nick depresses the buttons on the telephone, cutting off the connection. He will explain this to Peg later, if he sees her again. With his left hand still clutching the receiver, he brings it close to his chest, sinking back to sit on the bed. The feeling that pulses through his body elevates his spirit so that he barely wrinkles the bedspread beneath him. This racing surge, this clear emotion, will be called redemption. He has made contact.

Mirrors

ERIC IS keeping busy, in the time he has left. He's emptied the crumb tray of the toaster oven, polished its glass door and chrome top and, with the Windex out, he works on the large mirror by the telephone.

He lets the phone ring a second time before he lifts the receiver.

When Barb says, 'We have to talk,' Eric hears, 'You have to listen to me.' But he's done listening. As soon as he recognizes her voice, he interrupts her, with all of his own good reasons.

'You can't do this,' she says. 'You can't just fade away like this.'

Haircut, he reminds his reflection. An odour seems to be coming from the holes dotted over the phone's mouthpiece. He sniffs at these, then exhales into his cupped palm, checking.

'What's that noise? Are you getting a cold?' Barb asks.

Eric, tempted, considers bed rest, poached eggs on toast, flat ginger ale; a child's comforts. He says, 'I'm fine.' But he's weakened. 'Look, I'm meeting Ken about six. You could join us.'

'Let's get together for drinks?' Barb makes this sound like an oft-quoted refrain. 'You really can be a bastard.'

WITH THE plastic apron low and tight on his neck, Eric can see, reflected, the hot-wire look of his tracheotomy scar. The salon lights emphasize the damaged tissue. He shifts his focus. Men with their hair tightly wound around pink and white rods; this still looks strange to him. Eric has worn his hair the same way, with a part just to the left of centre, for as long as he can remember. Some years it's longer over the neck, shorter over the ears, but the part remains constant. Possibly there is even a smooth line on his scalp where the hair, discouraged, refuses to grow.

'We have no trouble making little wings, do we?' The stylist rakes his fingers through Eric's hair, pulls it up and back.

'I guess not.' Eric is uncomfortable under this touch. His eyes return to the scar. At seventeen he had rushed home to wolf down a hot dog before running back to school for a soccer game. The hot dog, loaded with residual antibiotics, triggered a violent reaction: Eric dropped into anaphylactic shock. At the hospital a young resident grabbed a knife from a tray of silver instruments and, quite literally, cut Eric's throat.

'DON'T DO IT,' he'd said, but only after Barb's breathing assured him she was asleep. He'd exhausted every serious argument in him and, finally, suggested, 'Why don't we have it first? Then if it gets in your way, if it cries or spits up on your clothes, then you can kill it.' She locked herself in the bathroom. Eric stayed in the living room, watching a rerun of *Barney Miller.* In September he starts his first full-time job. Teaching high-school history, admittedly, is small potatoes compared to practising The Law – that's how Barb makes it sound: *The Law* – so he doesn't know how he would feel if the choice were personal, only his. He can lack some essential confidence in his own enthusiasms: he has a model for his own hesitance. There was a day when he'd been home from school, legally, yet in the morning when he'd first heard the knocking at the door he imagined a blurred authority figure was at the house to declare him truant, someone not knowing about his school's professional development day. Possibly he was the victim of some elaborate trick; maybe there was no day off at all. In his early teens, his strongest sense was of his own powerlessness. He opened the door, a thin connecting line where *inside* met *outside,* and looked, expressionlessly, at the woman on the porch.

'I hate to inflict this on you,' she said, skipping past any preliminaries, 'but I think it counts as an emergency.'

'Yes?' Eric was cautious. At best, he might be expected to buy something.

'I broke a cap and my dentist said he'd see me this afternoon, but I have to leave now and the sitter hasn't shown up yet.'

'You want me to babysit?' Eric had just noticed the small girl at the woman's side. He stepped back, pulling the door wide open. 'Of course, I can do that.'

'I could leave Elly here, but the sitter's on her way. Do you see? If you could just stay at my place until she shows up.' The woman smiled, revealing that she had, indeed, broken a cap. The filed remnant of her own tooth was an ivory line in a chalky surround, bordered by white porcelain. Eric pulled his wind-breaker from the hall closet and followed the woman and her daughter across the back lawns, not locking the door behind him when he left his father's house.

Eric felt large and clumsy in the other house, and was overly cheerful when he spoke to the little girl.

'Well, Elly, can you write your name?'

'Yes, stupid.' The girl looked up from the paper she was cray-oning. 'I can do that.'

'Don't call me stupid,' Eric cautioned automatically, while she printed in large orange letters. He reached down for the page. 'Let's see. Elspeth?' he read, shaking his head. 'I've never heard of such a name. No, your name must be Elizabeth.' He took the crayon from her soft hand and printed that name, carefully mak-ing the two Es the same height, to teach her humility. He held up the sheet of paper so she could see, smiling in a way he hoped would convey the idea education was a pleasant thing, that she should delight in this correction. The little girl stared past the paper to his face, her eyes widening in an expression very much like terror.

'AND ALL DONE,' the stylist says, unpinning and shaking out the apron. Eric's hair falls to the floor and loses itself in the hair already there, waiting to be swept away. 'Tell Rosanne that's just a cut. But, really, I could do great things with a body wave.'

'I don't think so, thanks.' He pays the receptionist twenty-two dollars, getting change from a five to return with two singles for the stylist, one for the woman who washed his hair.

On the street, Eric intercepts messages that may or may not be meant for him. *Garbage* is stencilled on the side of a canvas tote bag, defining its contents, or the attitude of its owner, who also wears a sweatshirt to let him know *The Moral Majority Isn't Either.* Behind her, a man exits the record store, flashing *There Is No Gravity the Earth Sucks.* A man stepping off the bus (not the one Eric is waiting for) advises *Nuke the Whales.*

Two men on the sidewalk – a couple of men, with cropped hair and skin that looks cared for – are wearing very short, very tight khaki shorts, and white T-shirts with the sleeves cut off. *Bend Over I'll Drive* and *Sit On My Face and I'll Guess Your Weight.*

A blast of air-conditioner exhaust touches Eric, pokes into the spaces exposed by his haircut. He turns away, looking down the street from the bus stop. A crack, perhaps a foot wide, appears in the edifice of a six-storey office building and spreads, jagged as lightning but black, like a special effect in a low-budget film. There is something obviously artificial about the scene; it can't be happening. Things do not fall apart so easily. He looks around, to see if anyone else is noticing this. When he looks back, the building is halved, a ganglia of twisted girders reach across space, sections of floor and wall drift, scattered as sparrows. Then sirens cut the air, the sidewalk crowds with people – more pushing to see than running to safety – cars screech to a halt. A cloud of dust and grit slaps into Eric.

He steps back out of the chaos, through the revolving door of a department store. Inside, on the second floor, he buys fluffy bath towels in blue, green, orange and red. When he's signing the charge slip, his hand suddenly fists. The ballpoint pen cuts through the flimsy paper. Startled, he glances up at the cashier. The woman is wearing a parka trimmed with white fake fur. The store is having a 'January-in-July White Sale', which would explain the seven-foot stuffed polar bear he passed at the top of the escalator. Nothing of normal size happens in his life, nothing as simple, even, as having his dog run over by a truck. Instead, it was, 'My birthday puppy was married to the driveway by a four-ton pickup.' Like that, the pathos could be overwhelming.

His mother tells a story that, through repeated hearing, exists in Eric's mind with the strength of memory. His perambulator had been one of the old British style, very dark blue with a collapsible shade bonnet rather like the hood of a convertible car. Opened up, the bonnet created a cavern half the length of the pram. One morning in the park a small bird, a chickadee or a common lark, had flown into this space, circled once, twice, and then had flown off. This happened in less time than it took for Eric's mother to have any reaction at all.

Eric had told this story in his Autobiography as History seminar. There had been a moment's silence – appreciative, he'd thought – then the rest of the class pounded on their desks, chanting in unison, 'Revisionism. Revisionism.'

But Eric thinks, even at the age of eleven months, this is something he really would remember. Who could forget? Eric can close his eyes and feel again the soft touch of feathers, the feel of a wing brushing his cheek.

'ON PERSONALITY TESTS,' Ken tells him, 'eighty-five per cent of the population check *Yes* in response to "I think I am more sensitive than other people."'

'Really? That breaks my heart.' In the past, Eric has been told with similar authority that yellow is often a favourite colour choice of schizophrenics, that three times as many women as men attempt suicide (although three times as many men succeed), and that imagining peculiar odours can be symptomatic of a brain tumour. Ken is a psychologist. Eric makes Venn diagrams on the tabletop with the damp bottom of his glass. Set. Set. In the middle, where the circles overlap, a subset. He shakes his head sadly then, sly, he suggests, 'Maybe I'm equally sensitive, but to more things.'

'You're hopeless,' Ken laughs.

'But not despairing. Aren't you supposed to give me unconditional positive regard?'

'That's a professional service, you have to pay.' Ken has his sunglasses in his hands, snapping the stems open and closed. The plastic clicks like spike heels on a marble floor. He slides them on, his profile to Eric. 'Here she is.'

Barb is wearing a short skirt, coloured stockings – green, like zucchini is green – and a loose top made of something like cheesecloth. She looks like a woman in a magazine, Eric thinks; the kind of magazine with large, slick pages you might press against your cheek if you were reading in an overheated room. She sees them, and manages to turn her slight start of recognition into a wave.

While she's crossing the room, Eric moves his bag of towels to the chair beside him.

'Where I can see you,' he says, pointing across the table. He smiles. In Ken's mirrored lenses he can see himself reflected, twice. His forehead is large and pale; the room is convex, darkening behind him. He looks like the astral fetus at the end of *2001: A Space Odyssey*. The space baby.

'Nice to see you, Ken.' She looks down into the seat of the chair before smoothing her skirt against her thighs and sitting.

'What are you drinking?' Eric asks. A waiter has come to see 'what the lady would like.'

'I don't know. Nothing.'

'We can't have that. I'm having Ne Plus Ultra.' He turns to the waiter. 'Another.'

'I'm fine,' Ken says. He holds up his daiquiri as proof.

'Sparkling water, then.'

'At least,' Eric says, after the waiter has left. 'Ne Plus Ultra is what I'm ordering. I don't know what I'm getting.'

'What you're getting,' Ken says, 'is paranoid. Why wouldn't he give you what you want?'

'Beats me.' He scrapes his thumbnail over the arm of his chair. 'Perhaps Barb could tell you?'

'Just a minute,' Ken takes off his sunglasses. 'Do I detect some hostility here?'

'Never mind.' Barb shakes her head. 'That wasn't fair.'

'Fair!' Eric's palm slaps down on the tabletop. Peripherally, he is aware of heads turning, and he looks behind him, as if he's also heard a loud noise. Turning back, he says, 'Fair? Who told you to expect fair?'

'I do sense some tension here. You're not going to have a fight now, with me here, are you?' Ken keeps his glasses in his hands, but opens the stems. 'I couldn't cope.'

'We're not fighting.'

'Well, you shouldn't. Not you two. Some people just don't know who they belong to.'

'What did you say?' Barb turns from Ken to Eric, her mouth a narrow line, her eyes round and dark. 'What is he saying?'

Eric raises his hands, needing them to explain. At that moment his vision dims, the room recedes to a murky, twilight gloom. 'Oh, Jesus!' He waves a hand in front of his face. His fingers are a blur. 'My eyes! My eyes!'

'Sir?' The waiter is at his side, carrying a midget bottle of Perrier and two glasses on a cork-bottomed tray. Eric has only a moment to wonder at the clarity of these details before the waiter reassures him, 'We turn the lights down in the evening. For dinner.'

'Dinner?' Eric repeats. 'Oh, yes. Dinner.'

'I'll bring you menus.' The waiter backs off.

'Now we have to eat here.' Ken takes the short straws from his drink and slides them into the hair at his crown so they stick up like antennae. 'The young and the restless.'

'At least he called me "sir." '

'Damn fool.' Barb's voice is fond.

'Just stop that. I hate it when you understand me.' He pushes his chair back from the table and stands. 'Don't talk about me when I'm gone.'

THE MEN'S ROOM is down a flight of stairs beside the end of the bar. Over the polished mahogany planking, between the shelves of neon-bright liqueurs, a portable television is broadcasting, without sound, the evening news. He waits at the top of the stairs and is rewarded when a film clip of the collapsed building starts to air. He had been wondering if he had imagined the event, but a camera convincingly pans the wreckage. He waits for the screen to be filled again with a close-up of the anchorman before he starts down the stairs, thinking these should be by-lawed out of existence in places that serve liquor. Half-way down he has to put his hand out to steady himself, and he stops to stare at the wall, surprised he's left no trace of touch, no stain.

There is an ante-room in the space between the hall and the room of toilets and urinals. A leather couch is pushed up against the wall across from the row of sinks. One corner of this is ragged and a grey stuffing is showing, the material for a mouse nest. A newspaper has been left on the couch and Eric unfolds it over his lap.

Somewhere in the city, a ten-year-old boy is resisting being found. His photograph, in colour, dominates the front page of the weekend paper. This is captioned 'Tom Sawyer' for media reasons. Eric examines the picture, a posed, studio effort, checking the boy's shirt collar for signs of wear, signs of rough laundering. There's a long column of speculation by a police captain that the boy is a runaway rather than the victim of 'foul play'. Eric reads through a description of the boy's home life – the mother had dropped assault charges against the father in exchange for a trip to Disney World a month ago – and the phrase that comes to his mind is 'natural selection'.

In grade twelve biology, studying mitosis, he had stared at the cell division through a microscope, transfixed by the drama. He had focused into a tighter and tighter radius until all he could see were his own eye-lashes, magnified and prismed. Later, when Mr. Holmleigh ineffectually reduced the event on the four-by-eight space of the blackboard, Eric had asked what he thought would be a foolish and self-evident question. 'What makes it split?' He really wanted to know how the cell felt about the division.

'There are theories about environment,' the teacher started, not looking up at Eric, but down to the open text book in front of him. 'I don't know the why of it,' he confessed. 'It's an incredible accident.'

He tucks the sections, in order, against the fold. His cuticles are greyed with newsprint and he licks the ball of his thumb to scrub at them. He brings his hands up to his face to smell them.

In front of one of the sinks, he tugs up his shirt sleeves, holds his elbows against his ribs to keep his cuffs back, and runs cold water over his wrists. He looks up into the scratched mirror over the sink. The cells, each invisible to the naked eye, divide silently. Each division multiplies the mass. He imagines the cluster will now be about the size of a walnut.

'Mr. Holmleigh,' he says. 'You are a wise man.'

He is convinced, when it happens, there will be a visual clue. When the tumour is large enough, it will press against his optic nerve and he will have a blinding illumination before everything is taken away from him.

Cows

'A NIGHT on the farm?' Dave repeats into the phone. 'Are you propositioning me?'

'Not like that,' Heidi says. 'It is a proposition, though. Unless you're busy, I really could use a hand. Accept gracefully, if you're going to, okay? I'll make you dinner.'

Heidi's husband, Corbet, is on a business trip, and she needs help to feed the cows in the morning. Dave agrees to give this a try; he's never been to the farm, and he's hardly seen her since she started at teachers' college. After hanging up the phone, he moves around his apartment, getting ready. In the bathroom, he glances at his reflection in the mirror over the sink. He looks pale. He goes to the kitchen and, from the moulded egg compartment inside the refrigerator door, between the prescription vials of Mandrax and Fiorinal, takes a physician's sample folder of Tenuate. He breaks one of the caplets in half and swallows it dry. Diet pills make him sweat, but a half can keep him awake without making him speedy. He needs a little help; the day feels like it's starting over.

'Someone goes on a trip,' he says out loud. 'Half the stories in the world start this way.'

LIKE TIME-LAPSE photography, the sky starts to fill with stars as they drive farther away from the city. Dave stares out through the windshield of the truck and has a sense of the earth's roundness. On his right, trees create a solid wall of darkness. The starlight is intrinsic; it doesn't brighten the air or the ground. He touches the end of one finger to the glass, which is cold. In the light from the dashboard his hand looks cyanosed. Dave, at twenty-four, has as a hobby medicine and pharmacology. He's too old to be autistic, and aplastic anemia is unlikely, but for a few more years, he's in a major risk group for schizophrenia and multiple sclerosis. If – when – he gets through that, there's

Parkinson's and adult-onset diabetes. He thinks about these things the way some people think about the sex lives of others; there's a huge area between studied interest and personal involvement. Desire makes the difference.

They crossed the river half an hour ago, over the Champlain bridge, and are on a back road in Quebec. Dave's decided his economic boycott of the province (his protest against the new separatist government; they're not moving to separation quickly enough) won't be affected by spending the night on a farm. Dave doesn't imagine this will cost him anything. Between his feet, on the floor of the truck, he has a change of clothes and shaving gear in the satchel from Black Cat Leathers he uses as a book bag. He won't leave anything behind. Corbet is probably not to know he was there, anyway. They don't get along.

Spitting static, the radio loses its grip on the station. Bob Seger drifts away on Main Street, replaced by a sound like toothbrush bristles rubbed against a thumbnail, a sound that makes Dave want to yawn. Heidi reaches around the steering wheel to turn down the volume.

'Seger's such a loser,' she says. 'I like that album a lot. There're tapes in the glove compartment, if you want to look for something. In front of you.' She points.

'It's okay,' Dave says, watching her drive. 'This is nice.' Her hands are so tiny on the wheel. He'd been drinking at Raven's one night when she'd come in with some people from her French class. He left his friends and pulled a chair over to the periphery of the table where she was. At some point, when he wasn't responsible for his own actions, he grabbed one of her hands in his own and demanded, 'Look at this. I feel like I could make wishes with this hand.' For a moment, it seemed everyone in the bar stopped speaking and stared at him. Heidi asked, 'What would you wish for?' and he said, 'I'd wish I could undo this.' Then he felt he had to stay until the place closed, so no one would think he was backing down. That was when Heidi was sharing a house on the good side of Powell Street with Elaine and Paula. Paula was still seeing, off and on, a guy named Brian, with whom she'd lived for a year. Brian was a good friend of Raymond, Dave's older brother, who's in Morocco, a place Dave thinks has trouble written all over it: dysentery, hepatitis, maybe schizosomiasis. 'It's not the sixties anymore,' Dave told his brother. 'You don't lose the respect of your peers by going somewhere nice in 1977.' Their sister recently moved from Toronto to Edmonton; Dave doesn't include that, one way or the other; relocation is subject to a different set of rules. When he mentioned his brother's trip to Paula, not knowing who she was, she went to the basement and cried behind the furnace. Dave was tempted to follow her, asking, 'What? What?' but he didn't think anything would be accomplished by this. Heidi explained later: It was in Algiers that Paula and Brian had decided to live apart, then they couldn't make any changes on their charter flight back and had to sit thigh-to-thigh in economy class for nine hours. Dave struck himself on the side of the head. 'And everyone is supposed to know, to not mention North Africa?'

Like this, the connective threads between people make Dave think the world has been shrunk dry instead of blocked and pressed. Aside from Scandinavia and Australia, he has no intention of making himself known in more than the countries where he's already been. Maybe China; he could be faceless in a larger group. If singled out for any reason, he'd pretend to be American. Impersonation can have rewards other than anonymity.

'IT'S TOO DARK to show you some of the things I wanted to,' Heidi says. 'Remind me on the way back. There's some unbelievably tacky stuff along this road.'

'And you want to share it with me?' Dave turns to face her and points at his chest.

'Corbet takes it for granted. He thinks it's none of our business what these people do. None of *my* business.' Heidi laughs lightly. 'I'm talking about bathtub Madonnas, and lawn ornaments made out of bleach bottles. You're about the only one I know who'd appreciate it.'

'Well, thank you.' Behind the trees on her side of the road he notices flashes of blue-grey light, the unmistakable illumination of television screens. He hadn't considered there'd be a human population here. He believes the world is accurately depicted on maps, with blank areas between the dots indicating villages, towns, and cities, despite the logical conclusion it would then be possible to be *nowhere.*

'The bridge didn't wash out this year,' Heidi says. 'But it was up here that I totalled the Caddy.' The year she was in Dave's Faith and Atheism seminar she drove a yellow Cadillac, a strikingly inappropriate car for a student. They were older than the others in the class – she having taken time off school to organize a women's centre downtown; Dave for other reasons – so it was natural they would be aware of each other. One day, while the professor was trying to get them to appreciate the dynamic shape of a parable, using the Prodigal Son as his example, Dave shrugged off a question and said, 'I don't get it. I mean, it's perfectly obvious that the real story is the brother. What's his complaint, that he was denied the experience of waking up in a pig trough?' The rest of the class looked apologetic, at this waste of time, but Heidi stood up and applauded.

'It must have been exciting,' Dave says, about the car wreck. Under the truck, the bridge rattles, less than a foot above the water. Lights are strung over the road on the kind of poles that have disappeared from the city.

'I slept through most of it. If I hadn't been so tired I would have gone the long way around. But, yes, waking up in a sinking car was a trip. Corbet was a little annoyed.'

'I can imagine.' What Dave can imagine is having a heart attack and dying on the spot. There wouldn't be water in his lungs when his body was recovered. He reaches down between his legs and pats the satchel. When Heidi first moved to the farm, before she married Corbet, he'd tried to think of something to say about her new status, a comment to register the change. She called herself 'a farmerette.' 'I guess you have a lot of barn kitties,' he said, thinking he might offer to take one. A cat would be nice to come home to. Heidi said, 'They've been coming up to the house and hanging from the screen door. I might have to shoot them.' Dave had nothing to say to that, no answer at all.

The truck turns. Small pebbles ping against the underside and fenders. Heidi beats the heel of one hand against the steering wheel, keeping time, and she starts to sing 'Love Me Tender.' Her voice is deep and true and heartbreaking. Dave's throat seizes and he can't catch his breath. He closes his eyes and immediately opens them wide. Nothing changes, he's being carried through time and space, but even as he wills himself to memorize the moment, he feels it slipping away and he's left with a huge blankness.

'Sorry,' Heidi says. She pushes her hair back from her face. 'I get a little carried away on this last stretch. We're almost there.'

DAVE WAITS to make sure the toilet has flushed properly before running water in the sink to splash his face and hands. Vague details about septic tanks surface from the back of his mind. In the spring, they should be fed a mouse, to aid the chemical decomposition. Lacking a mouse, the acceptable substitute is one-half of a mole. Or, in extreme circumstances, a quarter-pound of ground beef. How he knows this doesn't engage him; his head is stuffed with knowledge for which he has no application. He switches off the bathroom light, follows the hall past the room he's been given, and goes downstairs to the kitchen.

Heidi is stirring something in a shiny nickel saucepan. Dave has never seen a pot so bright. The whole kitchen is stellar, not at all what he would have expected in a farm house. Almond-coloured cabinets slide forward at the gentlest tug, exposing plastic-covered racks like drawers, with the sides open for access. The yards of counter are surfaced with something that looks like marble, but is actually a synthetic material impervious to household damage. 'The salesman handed me a lit cigarette and said, "Go ahead, stub it out,"' Heidi said. 'Maybe,' Dave suggested, 'he only wanted to see if your mother raised you right.' There's a microwave, flush with the wall, mounted beside a real oven. A *conventional* oven, Dave corrects himself, as though he's learning the language of another country.

'Anything I can do to help?' He climbs up on one of the stools across from her. The counter into which the stove elements are sunk makes a bar in front of him, an island between them. Dave imagines himself doing something like peeling an avocado, slicing a lime; he should be wearing pleated wool trousers instead of jeans.

She looks up at him, the spoon raised to her mouth to taste. 'What I'm supposed to do now,' she says, 'is get the chicken out of here so I can reduce the liquid and add this.' She holds up a waxed carton of heavy cream. A blue and orange cow winks at Dave. The supermarket package is familiar.

'You could pour it through a strainer.'

'Good idea.' She takes a stainless-steel colander from one of the cupboards, puts it in the sink, then crosses back to the range for the saucepan. Dave watches her, thinking, What is wrong with this picture? He lets his eyelids droop, his mouth slacken. He's seen his reflection, wearing this expression, caught in daydreams. He calls it 'my impersonation of a minor appliance.'

'There, that's done.' Heidi returns to the range, the saucepan in her hands. Rising steam has damped the hair at her temples. She bites her lip. 'The stock went down the drain.'

'Yes?' Dave takes a moment to catch on, then pushes himself away from the counter, spins a complete circle on the stool. 'My good idea,' he laughs.

Heidi peers into the saucepan. Her tragic expression dissolves, and her laughter joins his. 'It'll be in the river by now.'

'The river. The river.' Dave is hilarious.

'The Atlantic Ocean.'

'I must take responsibility.' He raises his hands to the height of his shoulders, with his palms facing her. 'This is my fault.'

'Oh, please. Don't make excuses for me.' Heidi tosses the spoon across the room, into the sink. It strikes the colander with a metallic clang. Dave brings his hands down to his knees. She opens a door at the side of the counter island and lifts out a bottle of wine. 'You think I'll be able to get this open without shattering the cork?'

'I couldn't,' Dave says. 'I only get the stuff with a screw-top.'

Heidi gets glasses from another cupboard. Passing the sink, she glances in and says, 'I might be able to salvage some of that chicken, but it won't be what I planned on.'

'I'm really not that hungry.'

'Don't be polite. I said I'd feed you, just give me a few minutes to stop feeling incompetent.' The cork slides easily from the bottle and she pours wine for them. 'Let's sit in the other room.'

'You lead.' Dave stands, holding his wineglass. 'I wasn't being polite,' he adds. 'I took half a Tenuate earlier.'

'I don't know how you get diet pills. You can't weigh more than a hundred and seventy pounds.' Heidi passes him and he turns to follow her.

'One fifty-five, thank you. It's who you know.' He passes through the arch into the living room. 'Good God,' he says, then whistles. 'You have a projection television.' The Mylar screen dominates one wall of the room; the console sits in the middle of the floor, between two leather arm chairs. The far wall is lined with matte black shelves of stereo equipment. 'You didn't tell me.'

'It's Corbet's.' Heidi sinks into one of the chairs. There's an end table where she puts down her glass.

'This is the first time I've even been in the same room as one of these.' Dave squats down on his heels and examines the console. His own television is a twelve-inch black and white portable; he lived without one until PBS started rerunning *Upstairs, Downstairs.* His knee pops when he raises himself to sit in the second chair, facing the screen. 'Come in, mission control,' he says. 'This is command centre.'

'Right, I know,' Heidi says. She rolls her wineglass against her cheek. 'It's not exactly homey and warm, is it?'

'It's terrific. I could learn to live like this.'

'Well, I can't.' Heidi gets up and stands in front of the shelves. She raises the acrylic cover of the turntable and angles her head to read the label of the record there. 'Ronee Blakely?' She pushes buttons, flips switches, turns dials. Lights in blue, yellow, and red glow against the matte black shelves. Dave is impressed, even before the rooms fills with the clearest sound he's heard. He has the same album and he doubts he'll be able to listen to it again on his own system. Before the end of what Dave calls 'the young man song', Heidi returns to the kitchen for the bottle of wine. She sings, with the record, 'You're not the only man I know.' Dave moves down to sit on the floor, his back against the back of the chair. He's facing sliding glass doors with dark shapes beyond.

'Is that the north forty?' He points, then holds out his glass.

'West, actually.' Heidi puts the bottle beside him. 'That's where the sun sets.'

'And it's yours as far as the eye can see?'

'I guess so, I never thought about it. There're hills at the end of the property. You really can't see anything at night.'

'No.' Dave squints. 'It's like one of those movies where the camera moves through the woods with amplified breathing on the soundtrack.'

'Starring Patty Duke Astin? Or Elizabeth Montgomery? I know exactly the kind of movies you mean. Made-for-television. Tuesday night at the movies. I never used to understand how women could put themselves in those victim positions. Right from the opening scene, you know, with dust rising around a station wagon on a road in the middle of nowhere, I'd think, Come on, lady, don't do it. Run away. God, a *child* could see the place was trouble.'

'Yes, yes,' Dave agrees. 'And you get glimpses of her through the windshield, it's shadowed by trees, mostly, and she has this look on her face like she's just been released from some kind of institution.' He widens his eyes, wonder-struck, and takes a mouthful of wine. 'In fact, there's one where she *has* just been released from an asylum. His mother moved into the house when she was committed and doesn't intend to move out.'

'The incest motif.'

'No, before that got trendy. I think it was your basic family homestead story. No room for outsiders. Come to think of it, it is a kind of incest motif. But you'd think the woman might have caught on when the mother-in-law wore black to the wedding in the flashback.'

'Blinded by love,' Heidi says. 'She only had eyes for him.'

'Give me a break,' Dave snorts. 'What happened to *run away?*'

'Well, I'm here, aren't I?' Heidi picks up her wineglass. 'Let's see if we can do something about dinner.'

'I'm game,' Dave says, then laughs. 'Did I just make a joke?'

HIS HANDS have stopped shaking. The codeine he took before eating has masked the reaction between the wine and Tenuate, the synergistic effect on his blood pressure that made his temples pound like the sound of distant cannon fire. He raises his stubby glass of Sambuca in a toast.

'To country living,' he says. 'I think this place is really neat. This is the life.'

'You might change your mind in the morning.'

'What, in the fresh air and sunshine?' Dave's face is warm; he's well-fed and sleepy, enjoying the sensation too much to go to bed. 'Actually,' he adds, to be honest, 'I did bring a pair of dark glasses in case it was bright out.'

'That's better,' Heidi says. 'That sounds more like you. I didn't bring you out here so you could be sentimental, with some romantic ideas about the rustic life.'

'I wasn't accusing you of showing off. Is that what it sounded like? When you were in that house on Powell, I used to think, wow, there's the modern woman.' He raises his hands to put *modern woman* in quotation marks. 'Except for Paula being suicidal over Brian, you were so independent and –' He searches for the word. 'Focused. Like you were doing exactly what you wanted to be doing. You were a little scary.' An expression Dave takes to be hurt ripples over Heidi's face. 'Hey, listen,' he says. 'I just mean I thought you'd *arrived.* Hit the top, the way I think I'm supposed to be the man in the grey flannel suit, if that's still a goal for guys. It's kind of reassuring that you wanted something else.'

'Something else?'

'Well, this.' Dave lets one hand flop at the end of his wrist. 'A husband who's a successful businessman, a place out of the city and, when you finish school, a real job with time off in the summer.'

'You don't believe I set out to get this, do you? The hobby wife on Corbet's hobby farm.' Her head is down and Dave has to lean over the table to hear her. She looks up at him and, louder, says, 'I wanted the same things you want.'

'Me? What do I want?'

'All the things you have.' Heidi stands up and starts pulling dishes towards her. 'Your own place, for one. Downtown. You can go anywhere and do anything whenever you like. You don't have to plan your time to the last minute, or make excuses to anyone.' She slides the Sambuca bottle to his side of the table. 'More?'

'Thanks. I can do that?' Dave fills his glass, but leaves it on the table, admiring the clarity of the liquid. He tips his head to the side. 'My life sounds wonderful. I'm a fortunate fellow. I must be very happy.'

'Probably you are.' Heidi turns to carry the plates to the counter.

'Let me help you.' Dave raises himself to his feet. The action seems to take a long time.

'I'm just going to put them in the dishwasher.'

'Well, of course. The dishwasher. I should have known.' Dave sits back, moving his body to rediscover where the chair's been warmed by his own heat. 'Can we play with the toys in the other room some more?'

'Maybe for a while. We should be thinking about getting some sleep. Morning comes early around here.'

'Yes?' Dave glances at the clock on the microwave. After a

moment, the blue lines resolve themselves into numbers. 'Then I should pop a Mandrax now. They take about forty minutes to kick in.'

'I don't know anyone who's still doing drugs the way you do,' Heidi says. She carries the remaining dishes to the counter, leaving her liqueur glass on the table. 'I mean, Corbet does coke with his business cronies, but he lies about it. He starts sniffling in the morning, so I'll think he has a cold, then he comes home wearing out his back teeth. Like, I'm really fooled by this.'

'They're not *drugs*.' Dave spreads one hand over his chest in a protestation of innocence. 'I haven't even smoked grass since 1972.' He's proud of this. He tells people, 'I never again want to wake up facing the words *gunstock walnut*,' meaning the underside of a coffee table. 'These are pharmaceuticals. I get these from a doctor.'

'You must have done some shopping around to find a doctor who'd write a prescription for diet pills.'

'Actually, I just went to our old family doctor when I had an ear infection.'

'Okay.' Heidi returns to the table, sitting across from him. She takes the bottle and refills his glass, tops up her own. 'I won't sleep until I hear this. Start at the beginning.'

'It was when I got back from England, the first time. I was about nineteen. You know, when your feet hurt, you can lie down. But a pain in your head? You can't get away from it.' Dave cups his hand against the side of his head. The gesture is protective and familiar. He took the stool Dr. Pedersen indicated. The doctor pulled up a second stool close to his side. 'I thought you were going to be a little fellow,' he said. 'How tall are you now?'

'Five-ten, eleven, around there,' Dave guessed, unable to remember what he'd put on his passport. For some reason, he felt he was in the office of his high school principal. 'This ear started to bother me on the way back.'

'Where'd you go?' The doctor's breath stroked the side of Dave's face.

'England, mostly.'

'England. Don't you think London just reeks of sex?'

'I thought it was kind of expensive.' He lifted one hand to point at his ear. 'Uh, this.'

'I think I could afford it. I don't drink or go to gay bars.' Dr. Pedersen turned as he said this, rummaging through a tray of silver instruments and holding up what looked like a flashlight with an egg-cup on the lens end.

'This ear feels –' Dave turned slightly on the stool, only inappropriate words coming to mind. The doctor put a hand on his shoulder and peered into his ear through the instrument. It seemed to be at body temperature; Dave barely felt it.

'Just a little infection. Probably you had a cold coming on and it got pushed up in the plane. Some antibiotics will clear it up.' He patted Dave's shoulder as he stood. 'I'll write you a script.' He pushed his stool back so he could twist around and write on the desktop. When Dave reached for the paper, the doctor added, 'You look terrific. Lean. Do you diet?'

'Me? No, I don't have that kind of self-control.'

'Well, you would with these.' The doctor slid open a cabinet beside the desk and took out a clutch of orange folders, which he stacked up. 'I can give you samples.'

Dave started taking the folders from the desk, automatically, the way he'd take a pamphlet from someone who approached him on the street. They made an awkward handful. 'Do you have an envelope or something I can carry these in?'

'He said, "Why don't you just carry them in here?" and sort of patted at the front of my jeans.' Dave stands up to illustrate this to Heidi. He looks down at himself. 'I guess he meant the pockets, but I can't even get change into them without tearing skin off my knuckles. Now I wear a jacket with lots of pockets and he opens up this cabinet of samples when I come into the office and says he has to go get my file, so I'm alone in the room.'

'That's a little weird.'

'It is, isn't it? I never told anyone about it before.' Dave looks down at the table. 'It feels funny, like I've betrayed him now.'

'Well, that's because you have. He did set it up so it would be a little awkward for you tell anyone.' Heidi takes the glass from in front of him, clearing the table. 'But I'm not going to pass it on or anything. I'm glad you told me.'

'I guess I wanted to tell someone. Not the medical association or my mother, you know, nothing like that. It's just that I keep wondering, What kind of person does this happen to? Sometimes I'll be walking down the street and suddenly wonder what other people are seeing, and it's all the same feeling. I'm going to be fifteen years old for the rest of my life.'

'Don't start thinking it's your fault. He's the authority figure in that situation, even if you encouraged him in some way.'

'I don't see how I could have. I don't think being in pain would make me attractive to anyone.' He pushes his chair under the table. Heidi waits for him to be at the bottom of the stairs before she switches off the lights in the kitchen. Dave is half-way up when he thinks to turn back into the darkness and add, 'He has a beard.'

ON THE narrow bed, Dave relaxes into a natural, curled position. There had been a special night, when he was child, sometime between the first day of school and the Christmas holidays, when his smooth cotton sheets would have been replaced with soft, tickly flannelette. Year after year he had been surprised by this, as by an unexpected present. It had been a personal revelation, those flannelette sheets more pentecostal than any evidence the world was running according to plan; the first snowfall that blurred the hard angles of the city; a crack in the earth where a crocus was beginning its upward search for spring sun; that moment in the autumn when he noticed, sprinkling through the living green of the trees, the bright colours of decay; vermilion, scarlet, gold.

He wakes once. The sheet is tangled in a thick knot around his feet. He kicks, feebly, to free himself, but the effort exhausts him and he slips away until the air in the room is pale yellow and he hears a *whoo-whoo* from outside the window. Footsteps sound in the hall. He swings his legs over the bed and reaches for his jeans. He waits until he can hear Heidi in the kitchen before he goes to use the bathroom. For a moment, he debates swallowing a blue and white capsule, sparing a thought for his liver and kidneys, the demands put on them by drugs. He takes the Fiorinal. The trade-off is knowing how he will feel for the next few hours.

DAVE WATCHES the eggs puff up in the microwave. The process is remotely impossible, he thinks, despite the evidence. 'Some of the books say not to look,' Heidi told him, 'but I don't think you go blind or anything.'

'I heard an owl,' he says.

'Really? They don't usually come up to the house.' Heidi stands beside him, then taps the buttons marked Clear and Clock. 'These are done.' Dave steps back so she can open the door and move the glass dish to the counter.

'It went *whoo-whoo.*' He's not even close to duplicating what he heard.

'I think that was a dove. They nest in the eaves.'

'Well, what do I know?' Dave looks away. Any other time he's been awake at this hour, he's stayed up to it. He can feel the difference, between an ending and a beginning. 'I spend too much time flapping my lips to learn anything.'

'At least you talk. A lot of guys don't.' Heidi touches his wrist. 'I didn't want to have you trapped out here so I could whine about Corbet. I'd rather hear about you.'

'You would?' Dave narrows his eyes, considering the night before. His memory blurs into pastel strokes, the buzz of his own voice. 'No, you wanted to talk to me. I kept interrupting. Can you tell me now?'

'It's nothing. The everyday complaints of the average housewife. I know better than to think it's not boring. Even I get bored, and it's my life.'

'I'd hardly call you average.'

'No, *you* wouldn't. It's sort of too bad, isn't it? Thanks.'

DAVE FOLLOWS her to the barn. The ground is dark mud.

Corbet's rubber boots flop around his legs; the lumberjack shirt scratches his neck. 'Is that what you're wearing?' Heidi asked about his Frye boots and Viyella shirt.

'Yes, I planned to,' he said. 'What's wrong?'

She pointed, 'The boots, for one.'

'They cost two hundred dollars.' Dave looked at his feet. 'I had to go to the store three times before I could steel myself to write the cheque.' He managed to keep his own jeans, and his dark glasses.

There's a huge lean-to at the side of the barn, a single bracket in greyed wood. The top point of the sloping timber is about thirty feet high, slanting above bales of hay bound and stacked over the earth. Loose hay carpets the ground. The protected barn wall has a row of hinged openings that remind Dave of Advent cards, the paper window-flaps counting down the days to Christmas. Heidi puts her hand on the drop-latch of one of these.

'I'll do this one. It's the bull, and he's gone crazy.'

'Really crazy,' Dave asks, 'or just a little annoyed?'

'I mean insane. You can't trust him.'

'Shouldn't he be put to sleep, if he's gone nuts?' The phrase *mad dog* crosses Dave's mind. He can hear grunting and scraping through the wall of the barn.

'He's for breeding,' Heidi says. 'He doesn't have to think.' She moves to the next window.

Dave takes a step back and picks up a pitchfork. He hefts it in his hands like a baseball bat. He bends forward, the waistband of his jeans cutting into his stomach, and lifts some hay on the prongs.

'Like this?'

'About a hundred times that,' Heidi says, 'for one cow.' She opens the latch and pulls back the slats of the door. Immediately, a cow's head pokes out of the opening. Any softness suggested by the furred ears and large eyes is negated by the wet nose, the ropes of spittle dangling from the thick lips.

'Jesus,' Dave says. 'It's the size of a piano.'

'What were you expecting?'

'If you really want to know.' Dave sticks the pitchfork into one of the bales. He leans down and gathers some loose hay, about thirty stalks, and tucks it into the crook of his elbow. 'I thought I'd stand here like this,' he holds out some of the hay with his other hand. 'And say, "Here, cows. Come and eat."'

Heidi claps her hands together and laughs like a child. She drops down to sit on a bale of hay.

'That's great,' she says. 'You've been confronted with an unrealistic expectation. I wish I had a picture of you now, in those rubbers and that shirt. Poor Dave, this is no place for you, you don't belong here at all. You know, when I'm sixty years old, I'm going to remember you and really regret that we never had an affair.'

Dave takes off his dark glasses. The world lights up like a scene change in a poorly-edited film. Against the barn wall, the cow's head could be a trophy, stuffed and mounted. He presses the heels of his hands against his eye-sockets until his vision is filled with black and red spots. When he moves his hands, the spots remain for a moment, as a part of the real world he perceives.

'Sure,' he says. 'I'll look forward to that.'

An Act of Violence

TONY IS KILLING TIME. He wanders through the stores in the shopping complex of the building that, above ground, houses Evelyn's doctor. Upstairs, on the seventh floor, she is having examined a small growth on her knee, just where the skin dimples under the smooth curve of bone. Right at this moment, she's doing that.

'I'm sure it's nothing,' he told her, a week earlier, wanting to laugh at the picture she made, nude and supine on the bed, the reading lamp pulled close to the edge of the night table to angle the light over her leg as she pointed out this flaw to him. It was tiny mark, barely raised and only slightly discoloured, a weak-tea reddish brown. 'Maybe it's a bug bite or something?'

'Bug? What bug? No,' she shook her head, burrowing a snug nest into the pillow beneath. 'It's a rare type of cancer. I know it.'

Tony was about to suggest it might be a wart, but he stopped himself, knowing she'd rather have the cancer – her rare type would be, of course, easily treated – than a malady suggesting dirty little boys, or the ruined skin on a wino's nose. Witches had warts, not young women with promising careers in real estate. And it would not be, unequivocally, cancer of any sort. That had only been mentioned superstitiously. Evelyn takes these chances, second-guessing a greater power, assuming she will be rewarded with a lighter burden if she anticipates the worst. Tony worries that these chances, gambled and won, erode the odds in some unspecified future deal. There are no known rules by which to play this game. Mercy is an unmediated kindness; this is not predictable.

A DISPLAY has been set up in the wide centre mall of the underground complex. Cut logs are propped vertically into a fort-like fence, and over this is a large banner: DOUG AND ANGIE'S PETTING ZOO.

There are animals inside the pen: a small pig; a Shetland pony; some large birds like turkeys (one of these might be a pea-hen, dull and clueless-looking, abject); and a llama, its coat already heavily dandruffed with the sawdust spread over the floor of the confined area. In one corner, with its back to the walls, is a beast about the height of Tony's chest. Barrel-shaped, with a fluffy auburn coat, the animal has a strong, square face. There are two tiny horns, the colour of cheese parings, in front of its ears. The animal looks neither happy nor sad, content nor trapped, merely out of place. It needs to be somewhere other than here, and the choices may be too great.

'Hey,' Tony calls to a woman who is saddling the Shetland. 'Are you,' he glances up at the banner, 'Angie?'

'I am,' the woman answers, without changing expression, her hands continuing their work with the saddle. 'Want your picture taken on a pony?'

'Not today,' Tony says. 'This.' He points. 'Is this a buffalo?'

'That? No. That's a Scottish Highlander calf.'

'Oh.' Tony is curious about his own disappointment. 'Well, thanks then.'

He turns away and continues his wandering, ending up in a kitchen boutique, the kind of shop that specializes in appliances for persons like himself, those with a constant supply of small sums of money, a little left over after each month's expenses. Tony has heard this – having disposable income, more money than he actually needs – described as 'upscale' and rejected the word: 'middle class' seems to him a sufficient accomplishment. He even, sometimes, feels the urge to press an inventory on total strangers. 'This,' he would say, 'this and this. These things are mine.' He resists the urge; his pride is in achievement, not possession.

After much deliberation, tempted by a sleek pasta maker until he discovered the price of it – the decimal one point too far to the right – Tony settles on an electric coffee grinder. He's seen similar machines, but never one with such a vibrant plastic base, such an understated, clear grey acrylic top. This top doubles as a coffee measure and Tony, charmed, considers the appliance a fixture in his life. This new life, as he sees it, is composed entirely of Sunday mornings, drinking fine, expensive French roasts and working, in pen, the crossword from an out-of-town newspaper.

Pleased, he ransoms his car from the underground lot and circles the block, to be at the front of the building when Evelyn steps through the doors and onto the sidewalk.

She glances into the back seat before letting herself into the car, a habit Tony knows was drilled into her by her mother when Evelyn first started to drive. She is looking for rapists, he supposes, but why she should do this when he is in the car is not something he understands. Nor is it anything he questions: everyone is looking for something.

'What did you buy?' Evelyn asks. 'Something nice?'

'Coffee grinder,' Tony says, putting the car into gear and checking the mirror before easing back into the road. The traffic is dense, even at this late hour. 'Doesn't anyone work any more?'

'Never mind,' she says.

He turns to her, 'How about you?'

'Well, it's not cancer. I guess we both knew that, didn't we?' She waits for him to assent to this. 'What I have is something called, I think, dermatosis fibrosis. Something like that. I have it written down.'

'Sounds serious.' Tony lifts his foot from the accelerator.

'It isn't,' she shakes her head. Then she laughs. 'In fact, the doctor has three of them, these little bumps. He showed me. A perfect triangle.'

Tony lets the car reach the speed limit before he turns back to her, his eyebrows raised. 'And *where on* your doctor are these little bumps?'

'Don't be like that,' she says, putting her cool hand on the back of his neck.

'I saw a buffalo this afternoon. In the shopping centre.'

'You did? I don't think I've ever seen one, not in real life.'

'It wasn't really a buffalo,' Tony confesses. 'It was some kind of Scottish calf.'

'A Scottish calf is okay,' she says. 'It's no buffalo, to be sure, but it's okay.'

'It did look like a buffalo,' Tony says. Ahead is the turn-off, the street that will take them diagonally across the city to their apartment. He drops his hand to the indicator, then returns it to the wheel. 'We could just keep going, west, and see a herd on the hoof.'

'Like pioneers?' she asks. 'Or an early summer vacation?'

'God, I hope not like that,' Tony says. There had been a morning when he and his brother Ken had been awakened at first light to move through their own house like thieves. While their father loaded the car, their mother made breakfast for the boys. 'Finish the milk,' she told them. 'We can't take it with us.' Ken pushed his chair away from the table and stood with his back to the stove, watching his mother. 'Are you done? Then go and tell your father his family is ready.' Tony reached for the waxed carton of milk, filled his glass, swallowed and swallowed.

Outside the city, where the road had been blasted through rock, sheer stone walls rose on either side of the car. At impossible locations, where no man could reach, dark blue paint spelled out messages in giant print: I AM THE WAY AND THE LIFE and RAVENS 56. Tony, just out of first grade, moved his mouth over these words, unable to pose a question that would come close to asking what he needed to know. The last that he read, before the ground levelled and the roadside was merely forest, stated THE KINGDOM IS NEAR, muting him completely.

Even Ken, eleven that year, was quiet in the car during the long ride to the cabin. Their father, white-knuckled at the wheel, had repeatedly glanced at them through the rear-view mirror, saying, 'This is going to be fun,' in a disinterested, rhetorical tone, the voice that would ask, 'Have you done your homework?' and 'Why don't you share with your brother?'

'There'll be swimming and fishing,' their mother said, turning back from the front seat, holding her hair flat against the drafts and breezes of the car's ventilation system. She was wearing excitement like a new pair of shoes; maintaining her pleasure required she step carefully. 'Just look at that scenery.'

'It's pretty,' Tony said. The spring had been filled with whispers; their parents planning this, planning something. Framed by the car window, above the brown dust raised from the dirt road, leafy trees dissolved themselves into a solid block of shades of green, an expanse like the sky, wrongly coloured. He pushed his head back into the car's upholstery, dizzied by the car fumes, by the relentless vibration that blurred his vision. Even with his eyes closed, images jerked in and out of focus. 'Fun.'

The cabin was at the bottom of a narrow trail. Tony stood at the top, beside the parked car, a rolled air mattress on either side of him. His shadow on the ground in front of him looked like the shadow of three people. His father, lifting a cardboard box of kitchen utensils from the trunk of the car, suddenly fell forward, flinging the box away from his body. He stood, brushed at the knees of his slacks, then touched his chin where the skin was split, a thick bubble of blood swelling there. His hand was trembling. Around him, in an eccentric, static orbit, the earth was littered with gleaming metals; knives, forks, spoons.

'Already? Already?' Tony's mother hissed, white with rage.

'No, I tripped on something. A root or a stone. I swear it's only that. People can trip, can't they?'

Tony's mother walked over to examine the ground. Tony hoisted the air mattresses to his shoulders, they were no burden at all, and started down the trail, careful and hesitant. At the bottom of the cabin steps, his brother was sitting on his heels, using a twig to turn over stones set in the musty earth. Whatever he was seeing required all his concentration; his mouth was open with the effort, his lower lip glassy with spit.

Then, later, Tony was running down the wooden planking, arcing through the air to be caught and dipped into the lake by his father, who stood at the edge of the dock, his black nylon trunks ballooned above the water's level at the top of his thighs.

'Be careful,' Tony's mother called. She was sitting in the shade, on a plastic webbing chair, her legs propped in front of her on a Styrofoam cooler. A glossy magazine was open in her lap to a full-page advertisement of a woman in hat and gloves, high heels, and a long dress with a full, billowing skirt.

'I'm catching him,' his father said, lifting Tony back up on to the dock. 'Come on, get a good running start this time.' He turned and cupped one hand to splash a transparent crescent of water over Ken, who stood close to shore, knee-deep and immobile in the lake. 'Let's show her how to have fun.'

Tony propelled himself forward. The dock was warm and rough under his feet. He leapt and was unsupported until his father's hands, still strong, clamped to his rib cage. Tony faced into the land, trying to pick out his mother in the blur of colours, light and dark. In less than a year she would be gone. Sometimes, trying to remember her at this moment, he would picture instead the woman in the magazine, all dressed up and surrounded by empty white space.

On the way home, Tony picks up Guatemalan, Colombian, Mocha-Java, and Angolan black coffee beans. In the kitchen, he grinds a little of each of these, separately, for a taste test, while Evelyn fills out the warranty card in her generous, angular handwriting.

'I never thought of this,' Tony says, looking at the packages of beans, each white bag labelled with black grease pencil. 'It's like a list of repressive Third World regimes. Do you suppose we grow coffee here?'

'Those countries need to export,' Evelyn says. 'Or their economies would collapse.'

'Don't tell me that,' Tony says. 'I don't need the responsibility.'

'Nice,' he says, later, his hand cupped over her knee. 'That there's nothing wrong.'

'I want it removed,' Evelyn says, shifting her weight from his side.

'A little imperfection?' he grins. 'It's more interesting.'

'Don't be like that.'

'Like what?' Tony sits up, pushing the pillow between his neck and the headboard. 'You said your doctor has three. Why didn't he have his removed?'

'That's different.'

'A doctor doesn't take unnecessary surgery lightly?'

'It's not *surgery.*' Evelyn makes a face. 'It's a simple procedure.'

'That couldn't be done in a GP's office?' Tony suggests. 'It doesn't sound so simple.'

'Okay, so I have to go to a plastics man.' She raises her foot, pointing her toes. 'I know it's there and I don't want it to be.'

Tony keeps silent for a moment, trying to gauge her mood. Then, moving quickly, he seizes her wrists and pushes her down on the mattress.

'Confess, woman,' he leers, 'your doctor's bumps are where only his best friends would see them. Yes, yes?'

'Would you please let me up?' Evelyn lies under him like a stone. Tony, profoundly embarrassed, releases her. She crosses the room to the bathroom, turning back at the door to add, 'You're a crazy person.' Tony hears water running into the tub then, with a clanging of the aged pipes, diverted to hiss from the shower head before he says, 'Am not.'

He pictures her white skin, now pink against the real white of the bathroom tiles. Then he adds, 'If it's not broken, don't fix it.'

WHEN TONY was very young, one of the neighbourhood ladies, a Mrs. Audrey Darlington, achieved local celebrity by painting fish on her bathroom wall. 'She just picked up a brush and painted fish right on the wall,' his mother informed the family at dinner, her tone somewhere between astonished approval and smug reproach; she would never paint fish on her wall. But it was a measure of Mrs. Audrey Darlington's new status that the fish were mentioned to the husbands and children at all. Left to their own devices, it was entirely possible they might never have noticed; or, noticing, might have refrained from comment. What the women did was women's business, short of childbirth which occasioned a reluctant celebration, the excitement over the new-born vaguely clouded by the actual process of birth; rather a messy business, that, best to keep it from the men, protect the children.

Tony, precocious with new learning, pictured the fish as cartoons, similar to the decals only recently wire-brushed off his own bedroom furniture. He imagined a type of exotic carp, all silky dorsal fins and rubbery, pursed lips. Possibly heavily lashed, coy eyes. Orange, most likely, or a decorator's pink.

Playing with Nick Darlington one afternoon in the Darlingtons' yard, and needing to pee, Tony walked through their house and up to the second floor bathroom. Any house but his own was hushed and private – a museum – and even carefully aiming a yellow line at the side of the bowl Tony was properly diffident, silent. Finished, and zipping his jeans, he looked around to make sure his presence hadn't disturbed the room. There, on the wall directly over the guest towels, were the fish. Not at all the expected cartoons, these were two flat, grey perch, both facing the same direction. Each had a gaping, twisted mouth; each had one smooth, round eye, clouding with exposure to the air.

Mrs. Audrey Darlington had painted two dead fish on her bathroom wall.

'THEY MADE ME weak, those fish,' Tony tells his brother. They have come from the Cineplex to Little Eden, for a drink after seeing *A Woman Under the Influence*. (Earlier, Tony had been amazed to discover Ken had never seen this before. 'Man calls himself a psychologist,' he said, 'and he's never seen the best film about mental illness in the history of the world.') Now Tony is pontifical with insights, luminous with the possibilities in the story of his own life. 'I felt like I'd been confronted with the very nature of women, and that I would always be outside their world.

They had their own symbols, their secrets and creations. That's what I thought at the time. I remember.'

'I don't even remember being told about them,' Ken says. 'It's interesting you would.'

'You were older when Mom left,' Tony points out. 'It was only one of a greater number of episodes for you. Anyway, what I wanted to tell you was that later I thought I was wrong about being excluded. I decided that the fish were symbols all right, but symbols of the massive boredom of the suburban housewife.'

'A modern interpretation,' Ken nods. 'What can I say? You're an eighties kind of guy.'

'I'm not, don't say that,' Tony insists. He lowers his voice to make his point, speaking in a near-normal voice through the noise around them. 'I think changing my mind was wrong. An eighties adjustment, like you said. Those two fish were meant to be – what is the word I want? – *estranging*. They were there to beat Mr. Darlington over the head, and Mrs. Darlington wouldn't have to lay a glove on him. It was a cold war.' He leans away from the small table between them, unsuccessfully trying to cross his legs in the limited space. 'What do you think?'

'Idiot savant,' Ken says. 'The boy who understood women. How often have you seen this movie?'

Before Tony can respond, a man squeezing his way through the bar bumps their table. Tony's beer slopes to a high angle in its mug, but doesn't spill over. He looks up at the man, preparing to murmur 'No harm done' when an apology is delivered. But the man, instead, stops and looks back and forth from Tony to Ken, then to Tony again. His face, round and flushed, splits into a damp grin. Below this, his shirt collar is unbuttoned, his tie yanked loose, still knotted. The man is in his fifties, middle-management in a small firm, maybe retail sales – carpets or cars; not cameras or stereo equipment – or insurance. He's been here since work, say an hour after the stores closed, and he'll drive home, rather than take a cab or bus. This assessment comes easily to Tony, what Ken would call a 'value judgement.' But Tony has no feeling of superiority or malice; his observation is merely a short-cut that leaves his mind open to process anything beyond appearance. If he left himself always receptive, allowing everything to happen for the first time, he would be no better, he thinks, than an animal or a child, burned, who makes no association between *stove* and *hot*. Or, and he's said this about the cataloguing system used at the library where he works, 'If we don't keep it simple, we'll all overload and die.'

'You're brothers, right?' the man says. 'I could tell that a mile off, you being related.' He starts to laugh. 'A couple of white guys.'

'We are pretty pale,' Ken says in a reasonable tone.

Tony can hardly disagree. He and his brother have inherited hair the colour of rye flour, not blond but beige, and skin that makes them look like they were, in Tony's phrase, 'carved from a bar of soap'. The man continues to stand in front of them, hilarious as if there were some amusement they were sharing. Tony rolls his eyes at Ken, but his brother is looking up at the man, a non-committal but pleasant expression on his face.

'I think that's enough,' Tony says coldly. 'It's not like we're albinos or anything.'

'I didn't mean anything,' the man says, his contrition as rapid and, perhaps, as sincere as his humour had been.

'Yeah, sure. Why don't you just leave?'

The man shuffles off with some awkwardness, having to push his way through the people standing between the table and the centre bar. His shirttail has escaped his slacks at the back, and hangs below his suit jacket, a white revelation like the quarter moon.

'Christ,' Tony says. 'I really hate a friendly drunk.'

'You might have let him have his moment,' Ken says quietly. 'There are a lot of lonely people in the world.'

'So why don't they talk to each other? They don't have to go around making me feel like a target.'

EVELYN MADE a killing a few months earlier, and unloaded a huge, unsaleable house, very nearly a mansion that while on the market had been divided into four or five apartments. The buyer, according to Evelyn, has spared no expense in re-converting the place into a single residence; knocking down walls, ripping out superfluous kitchens, soliciting advice from no fewer than six architects on bathroom designs. Now the house is finished, and Tony and Evelyn are invited to the housewarming party.

'You must have heard of her,' Evelyn insists. 'Alicia Keating. She's practically revolutionized the cosmetics world. She has a new line of facial masques coming out in the fall, she told me.'

'How would I have heard of her?' Tony asks. They are dressing in the bedroom, an activity that usually co-ordinates effortlessly. But tonight, for some reason, he seems to be in Evelyn's way; she continually turns away from him, stepping to one side when he crosses the room to pull a clean shirt from the closet. Taking his cue from her mid-length, Laura Ashley skirt and blouse – her 'school-marm' outfit – he has decided on pleated wool trousers in a muted, autumnal weave, white shirt and tie, tweed jacket. 'Are we going to have to try the masques?'

'That might be fun.' Evelyn laughs. 'Just think of it, numbers of people walking around with this orange stuff on their faces. The ultimate anonymity. I'd better make sure I can remember what you're wearing, so I don't leave with someone else.' She steps back and exaggerates an appraisal of him, head to toe. 'Humn.'

'Remember that make-up seminar thing you went to? When you came home looking like a Shanghai whore?'

'A Shanghai whore! I did not,' Evelyn protests. 'I looked just fine, it was only the light in here.' She raises her arm to indicate the brass ceiling fixture. The move lifts her skirt over the tops of her boots. At the base of her knee, where the skin cups down to the shin, there is a white gauze pad, held in place by a large equal sign of pink adhesive tape.

'So.' Tony sits carefully on the edge of the bed. 'Did it hurt?'

'No.' Evelyn turns away from him, towards the dresser mirror. She pats at her hair, ruining the effect of several minutes careful brushing. 'Everything is just fine.'

'I wish you had been able to tell me,' Tony says. 'I wish you hadn't done it like this.'

'You'd have worried, or carried on. Besides, it was no big deal.'

'Letting someone cut you, no big deal?' Tony looks away. 'What'll you have now, a scar? That'll be better?'

'Just a little one,' Evelyn admits. 'This is something I'm responsible for, okay? And, yes, that's better.'

Tony sits with his hands open and empty in his lap, looking down. Mensal, heart, hepatic and brain – these are the lines of the palm, corresponding to destiny, longevity, health and profession. Ken would tell him that palmistry is naive and superstitious. Tony thinks the craft fits neatly into the tenets of psychology: you are born; you struggle, fail or succeed, against influences beyond your control, your fate; then you die.

'Don't you see the similarity?' Tony's asked. 'You just give people longer – what, the first five years of life? – to be irrevocably shaped.'

Ken disagreed, of course, 'What I teach, not give, is the knowledge of personal control. The *shaping* you mention is a dynamic process.' Tony had raised his hands to cover his ears. 'Stop it. Don't tell me it just goes on and on. That's the same as having everything happen all at once.'

The lines of imagination and generation are revealed on the percussion, or striking edge, when the hand is made into a fist. With some effort, Tony does not fold his fingers down, does not turn his wrist.

ON ALICIA KEATING'S verandah Tony and Evelyn stand side by side like the figures on a wedding cake, rigid and silent. The door is pulled open from the inside by a young woman who remains behind the oak and stained-glass panels as another woman turns to the door, crying, 'Evelyn, honey, usually I'm the one who under-dresses for parties!' It must be Alicia: the vivid woman surrounded by the wide expanse of foyer is quite possibly the most beautiful Tony has ever seen; creating her own cosmetics would be an instinct. Tony puts his hand on the small of Evelyn's back, for support, and she turns to him briefly with a look he can't decipher before stepping down to greet her hostess. 'Alicia, already I can tell that it's a masterpiece. And to think no one else even imagined the possibilities.'

'Oh,' Alicia is airily dismissive. 'It takes a special eye. One must have a vision.'

'Yes, yes,' Tony agrees too quickly, trying not to stare at the woman. He touches the knot of his tie, anticipating the evening ahead of him.

Introductions are hardly necessary: the architects are young-ish, new-school professionals in cleaned-and-pressed corduroy; the sub-contractor is slightly shorter, slightly heavier than the contractor; the escrow lawyer – a woman named Barb something – might have been unexpected had she not been so obviously dressed-for-success in a navy blue suit, white blouse and flat-heeled shoes. With the exception of a few neighbours (who must have been incredibly inconvenienced during the renovations, yet now appear benignly tolerant) everyone has some connection to the house, or to a person with that connection. Obedient to this connection, they move together in a roughly shaped mass.

Tony lets himself drop to the back of the group, joining the others who are 'with' someone ('And this is Tony,' he'd been introduced. 'He's with Evelyn, who found this when it was a pile of trash. Just trash.') as they climb the stairs, stand in the hall outside of rooms. Always a room behind Alicia's commentary, Tony leans against door frames, appraising the details to which attention is not called. There are no pictures to break up the expanses of wall: no ashtrays or books clutter the tabletops. The rooms are uniformly white, as sterile as a dentist's office, if not so well lighted. Tony scrubs his front teeth with a forefinger, then rubs his palms against his thighs. He counts five telephones and three televisions before he discovers any reading material and at that, charitably, he is giving credit to a slick Italian magazine of hairdressing designs. He rejoins the group outside the bath-room. Phrases are passed to him in quick, exclamatory gasps:

'Wall-to-wall,' and 'entirely mirrored,' and 'hand-painted, real bone.'

Human, Tony thinks, No doubt the bone is human.

The group of people reverses itself, and Tony is leading as they enter the dining room. He takes a seat at the far end of the table. The same woman who had let him into the house is now bringing the meal in from the kitchen. There is no seat for her at the table, and Tony is uncomfortable being served this way. He keeps his eyes averted, watching the others. From the corner, with his back to the wall, his view is unobstructed. He grips his wine glass in his hand, ready to cover the lower half of his face, already flushed by what he considers an embarrassment of food.

'Kiwis,' the lawyer coos. 'Craig's lamb,' one of the architects offers. And this is the table talk; most of the company too busy discussing the food to eat. Only the sub-contractor, his plate arranged in neat quadrants, devotes his attention to the task at hand with an enviable re-creation of manners; his isolation is a pleasure to watch. Tony chews slowly, not wanting to clear his plate prematurely, but the lamb fat congeals like soft frost on the china and he leaves as much as the man on his left, the woman on his right. By the time Alicia suggests they move to the living room for coffee, the table has a decided air of erstwhile massacre.

'There's a place here,' the lawyer says, patting the cushion beside her on the loveseat. She waits for Tony to sit, then holds out her hand, 'I'm Barb.'

'Tony,' Tony says, briefly taking then releasing her hand. 'I'm with Evelyn.'

'Evelyn? Oh, yes. The real estate lady. Do you have children?'

'I'm sorry?' Tony tilts his head, trying to understand the question. Then, 'No. We don't even have a cat.' Her expression remains the same, and he qualifies, 'We're not married?' to encourage her. After a silence, he asks, 'And you?'

'Me? No, I'm a lawyer.'

Tony glances wildly around the room until he spots Evelyn, bent forward to hear something the contractor is saying. He stares at the back of her head, willing her to look up and signal to him that it is time to leave. But an hour passes, more than an hour, before they are in the foyer, saying goodbye. Tony stands with his hands clasped behind his back while Evelyn makes the correct social noises. 'A real treat,' she says. 'Usually the sales just disappear into the ether. It's nice to keep in touch.'

'Listen,' Alicia says. 'I was glad for the dry run. I'm giving a party for my friends next month, and I wasn't sure everyone would fit.'

Tony amends the thought he had earlier: At least the bone is human.

SAFELY HOME, Tony stretches out on the bed and yawns hugely. 'I'm bagged,' he says. 'I feel like I've been assaulted.'

'Assaulted, what are you talking about?' Evelyn lets her skirt slide to the floor, bends over to pick it up. She crosses to the closet in her boots and nothing else, hangs the skirt from little loops inside the waistband, then sits on the edge of the bed to pull off her boots. 'What assault?'

'The whole evening. Didn't you feel a little abused? In the most hospitable manner, of course.'

'She's a very successful woman,' Evelyn says. She lets her boot drop to the floor, rolls down her kneesock.

'And success is another country?' Tony asks. 'The rules are different there?'

'No, of course not,' Evelyn shakes her head.

'I can't say I thought much of that house as a place to come home to.'

'But she must have worked very hard to get what she has. She deserves to enjoy it.' She raises her knee, peers at the bandage there, picks at one corner of the adhesive tape. 'I could learn to enjoy what she has.'

'Don't mess with that,' Tony cautions. 'You'll make it worse.'

'You know what?' Evelyn stretches out on the bed, pushing herself up with her palms to lie beside him. 'I think I'm going to have to sleep on my back. And you know what they say.'

'What do they say?' Tony lifts his weight up on his elbows. His underarms are damp.

'They say a change is as good as a rest.' She shows him a wicked grin and adds, 'Take your mind off feeling assaulted.'

'Yes,' Tony says. 'Really, my whole body feels like it's been beaten with a stick. Beaten with *chic.*' He moves closer to her, to narrow the range of his vision, allowing himself this distraction yet sure he will look back at himself with an imagination of motives, a familiar suspicion that control is being lent to him as a manipulation.

TWELVE DAYS later, when the bandage is removed and the stitches are taken out, Evelyn has a small, shiny mark, like a flattened and sideways 's' under an umlaut. Despite the finality of marked tissue, the permanence, a scar is no achievement. It is not a conclusion. A scar is half of a conversation, the probing questions asked by a stranger sharing the confinement of a travelling space, a bus or airplane: What past life is revealed by this? Who are you, to have been thus afflicted? How have you survived? Scarring, like physical perfection, invites prurience.

Tony is silenced by those two little white dots, where a sharp point pierced the skin. He's a man on the outside and he feels only a dutiful paternalism. The obligation defeats him – this is not his responsibility – and he hears his father saying, 'I won't be blamed. You and your brother walk around the house with those eyes, like two owls on a branch.' Tony shook his head, the movement imperceptible in the dimly lit living room, not wanting to hear this, not wanting to be seen hearing this. His father's voice was thick, each word a sullen, forced, sound, with a tremor that mimicked the palsy of his hands, the ineffectual grasping and releasing of the slack grey flannel of his trousered lap, as if something under the fabric was eluding his hold. 'What do you think I could have done, to hold her? You can't imagine what hatred she had for me, for ruining the future she'd planned. So she just left and started over. She didn't even leave me alone, to my own life.

Well, go try to find her, if being her son is a job you want to take on. I don't need you to worry about me.'

Tony leaned forward, into the cone of light from the lamp beside him, preparing a protest, but his father added, 'It's not that I ever wanted children at all. No, I never wanted them at all.'

Ken had warned Tony about these declarations; the clutching at autonomy was as symptomatic as the disease's progression, the slurred speech, the lack of balance, the unco-ordinated motor control. Tony would not believe, or even discuss, his brother's diagnosis. The man was recovering from a stroke, no more or less. He was not young.

TWO YEARS LATER, refusing permission for an autopsy, Tony says, 'I didn't listen to you then, and I'm not listening to you now.' They are in the parking lot of the hospital. Tony will not enter the building. Ken's face is rouged by the *Emergency* sign, as if lit from within the way it would be if he stretched his mouth over the lens of a flashlight, a thing Tony remembers doing when he was a child, many years ago. 'You want proof? Then what? I've done my research on this, Ken. The best we get is a fifty-fifty chance of not developing what you think he had.' Tony does not name the disease; he will not allow it that relevance. 'You think someone is going to come along and give you some kind of signed guarantee?'

'No, that's not the point.' Ken puts his hands into his pockets and leans against the hood of Tony's car. 'The stroke may have masked the symptoms. The diagnosis might be wrong. It's confirmation we're after, knowing what our own chances are.'

'That's fifty per cent each, Ken, not one of us or the other. We'd still wait it out alone. The laws of mathematics aren't about justice. Even randomness is predictable in its own way. No autopsy is going to certify you're entitled to your three score and ten.'

'It's better to know,' Ken says quietly.

'Is it? Always? Nobody can own the future.' Tony looks away, to where a small park is visible between the brick hospital buildings. There is enough natural light in the air to silhouette a low wooden bench and the frame of a swing set, the chains unseen from this distance. He adds, bitterly, 'This certificate is non-transferable.'

ON SUNDAY morning, Tony wakes early and pads quietly, barefoot, into the kitchen. At first he thinks the weak light is to blame, is blurring his vision, then he can tell that the coffee grinder is badly scratched. The inside of the cap, formerly smooth and shiny and clear, is now cloudy and rough, ridged with sloppy, non-concentric circles as if it had been clumsily sanded. He knows, even before the proof reaches his nose, almost as if he has been waiting for this information, that Evelyn has used the appliance to mince cloves. He stares at the grinder – worthless junk now, as far as he's concerned – not at all the sleek machine that had pleased him so much. He opens his mouth to call Evelyn and confront her with this, then leaves his jaw slack, remaining mute. The plastic is smooth in his hand; the violated interior is not evident to his touch. If he had less than his five full senses, this moment would pass without notice, exactly as would all the moments of the rest of his life. Such ease is – must be – false.

He must plan his escape, he decides, although he loses this conviction almost instantly, in the choice between *to* and *from*. A brief image of the gentle swell and trough of the Pacific Ocean fades from his mind and he returns to standing, barefoot, on his own kitchen tiles. In the intensity of his silence he becomes aware that the refrigerator has kicked into a low purring, the motor responding efficiently to task. His arm arcs back and swings strongly forward. The coffee grinder hits the side of the fridge with a disappointing sound of chipping plastic, no great explosive crack. Still, the pieces on the floor are obviously beyond repair.

Tony cannot quite manage a smile, his breathing is too wild, but he nods his satisfaction. He may never be home free but he is, for now, very much at home.

According to Plan

ON THE THIRD LANDING, Dave has to stop for a breather. He rests one hand on the banister, then pulls back and looks at his palm. The eight million stories of The Naked City are small change compared to the infinity of infectious microbes he imagines skinned over Manhattan like shrink-wrap. Dense populations breed their own possibilities for extinction. He'll have to remember not to touch his face.

He wasn't always so cautious. Fifteen years ago, the day after landing in Tel Aviv, he'd stuffed himself on *swarma,* a tepid meat – lamb? camel? – from a street vendor with pearl-cast eyes and fingernails blackened as the claws of an anteater. A friend gave Dave a card for his last birthday, his thirty-third: *You're only young once.* And, on the inside: *But it leaves you tired for the rest of your life.* Some truths can survive commercial sentimentalizing.

'Dave?' The voice sounds hollow and inhuman, bounced off the multiple planes of the stairwell. 'It's up one more.'

'A voice from the sky. Is that the Baby Jesus?' Dave asks, starting up the last flight, to the apartment Sara's borrowed for the weekend. Now he can see her leaning over a precarious-looking rail. Its base, at eye-level to him, seems to be no more than flakes of paint threaded with cobwebbing as substantial as cigarette smoke. He manages not to call out a warning, 'Move away. Get back.' Instead, he says, 'Living here would make joining a health club redundant. I can feel myself losing weight.'

'There're not *that* many stairs,' she says.

'Not for llamas, maybe. Or those other things, like goats. Ibexes?' He reaches Sara and, movement inhibited by the narrow hall, he gives her an awkward hug, his chin pressing into her temple. There's a quirky hesitation when he releases her – time for a mental check of the Index for Greetings (1980s), Men & Women, Previously Acquainted – a handshake might have been more appropriate.

'Don't let me complain about living in a split-level any more,' he says, stepping away. He raises a hand over his chest. 'My heart.' He means the real muscle, which must be enlarged, the chambers coarse-walled, by his intake of coffee and cigarettes. There may be scarring, as well. From nineteen to twenty-three, the years he calls 'my contribution to medical science,' his diet included regular snacking on Dexamyl. He was adding hours to his wakeful life, with purpose and contentedly; but when he was ready to call an end to the day, late, late-night television movies, tedious and numbing as they were, fell short of the tranquillizing effect he needed unless synergized with Seconal. And some mornings, first thing, he'd need a couple of Darvon for the pain in his jaws, from sleeping with his teeth clamped down as though his dreams were of conquering strong prey, tearing striated tissues, crunching thick bones.

On the birthday just past a friend said, 'Nobody who went to school with you ever thought you'd live this long.' He laughed, the light, social sound he makes when attention is paid to him, but he felt a split in the ground where he stood on his own patio, a maw of treachery. *And no one* did *anything?* he thought. *Things were going according to plan?*

INSIDE, on the right, there's a small, doorless room. Through the murk of absorbed light, Dave makes out a low, shallow sink. The enamel is netted with lines and chips, like an x-ray of osteoporous. A particle-board cabinet leans away from it, repulsed. The pathetic fallacy is alive and well.

'Did I come up the wrong way?' Dave asks. He pushes the door closed behind him, shifting the light from yellow to pale brown. 'Was there an elevator?'

'No, there's only one door. Why?'

'Nothing.' Dave follows her to where the area widens, past a rack of industrial shelving. 'Just, I wouldn't think the service room would be off the foyer.'

'You mean there,' Sara points back. 'That's the kitchen.'

'You're kidding!' Dave hears the note of real shock in his

voice and covers his mouth with one hand. Too late, he realizes it's the hand that touched the banister. He thinks: Exposed. 'Sorry. I didn't mean to be arch.'

'It's not *my* place,' Sara says. 'But if I lived in Manhattan, I'd be glad to get it.' She bends over an angled drafting table in the far corner. 'I should leave a note, in case Margaret comes back. She might have decided to take a later train and be running around organizing last-minute things.'

'Actually, it's ...' Dave looks around. The place is a nightmare: what it looks like, feels like, is a garage, one day in the spring when the city has announced a special garbage collection to rid tax-paying homes of shredded mattresses, gutted television consoles, springless sofas, burnt-out refrigerators and ovens; urban detritus gathered in one place to be finally, firmly, rejected. Before he can think of a word other than 'wretched,' one of the lumps in the corduroy couch shifts and regards him with a green-eyed level gaze.

'A cat.' He winks at the animal, a complicitous gesture, the same way he'd wink at a dinner companion in a restaurant where the staff revealed themselves overly familiar. At home in Ottawa he always says, 'Hi,' to the animals he encounters on the street, although he examines the sidewalk, or squints at the horizon, when confronted by a neighbour. 'This must be a nice place.'

'Margaret warned me not to touch her,' Sara says. 'She bites.'

'Do you do that?' Dave asks, trying to sound stern. The cat raises one paw, licks between separated toes. 'Well, then, no pats for you.' He makes a great show of turning his back. The wall he's facing is covered with enlarged black-and-white photographs and he leans forward to examine them. For a moment, he wonders if this inspection is in the same category as reading someone's mail, but the content of the photos reassures him the display is meant to be public. All the pictures are of one man, a shaggy, disreputable-looking type who, evidently, didn't receive notice when the Summer of Love came to an end. Not far from here, he realizes, on Macdougal Street, with the murder of Linda Fitzpatrick and her boy-friend, Groovy. Dave was, maybe, thirteen years old when this was on the news, and it's stuck in his mind with the images of a man walking on the moon, a woman in a pink suit sliding up and back out of a white convertible, a man rolling on the floor while a woman covers him with a blanket, reaches for the telephone. Mysterious as all the human senses are, memory is the one with fewest clues to function, to meaning. What is the use of this string of images?

The photographs might be very old, relics of ten or fifteen years but, Dave decides, surely their proper home is a large envelope, stuffed in a desk drawer.

'That's Timmy,' Sara says, moving behind him. 'Margaret's friend.'

'Timmy. Let me guess. Health food? Or pottery? No, wait, he designs non-competitive children's games.'

'He's a public defender.'

'Jesus, God.' Dave steps back from the photos, shaking his head. 'I'd float a bank loan to get private counsel.' There's a metallic rattling at the apartment door. Dave turns, focusing down the narrow tunnel created by the wall and the edge of the shelving, and sees a light-haired woman looking at him. Her expression is frightening, the face of fear, and he raises his empty palms to her, saying, 'No, no.'

'Oh.' Sara moves around him. 'Margaret,' she says. 'I was just leaving you a note, saying I was here. This is my friend, Dave. He's visiting from Canada.'

'Sorry about surprising you that way.'

'The door wasn't locked,' Margaret says. 'I couldn't figure out what happened.' She shrugs out of a light raincoat, while cross-ing the room, and flings herself down on the sofa. Immediately, she takes on the contours of a woman who's spent the day there, chain-smoking and reading old magazines. 'I'm only here for a minute. Timmy wanted me to pick up the kids.'

'We're on our way out, too,' Sara says. 'To the gallery.'

'Did you find the review? I left it out somewhere.' Margaret makes an abstract gesture. Dave can't tell if it's a dismissal of the review or an acknowledgement of the state of the room, but he's impressed by her attitude. He's also on edge, unable to think of anything to say. The room feels very small, and Sara is moving in a jerky, disconnected manner, matching the fragmented things she says, about how her bus was early, her husband's doing some necessary work around the house, the central location of Dave's hotel. The effect is dizzying; he has to leave his arms at his sides, straight down, to maintain a vertical posture. When Margaret gets up to see them out, he notices the cat, pressed into the cushion behind her, still curled in sleep. He sucks a wedge of his cheek between his molars and bites down.

'DID YOU see that?' Sara asks, when they're on the street, heading for Fifth Avenue through the thin, chilly rain.

'Her squashing the cat? I didn't think I'd live through it.'

'No, the word, in the air between us. Largest letters I've ever seen.'

'What word?' Dave, at the corner, puts his hand on her back, to move her past a group of men waiting for the light. He looks down the street for a cab.

'Margaret couldn't take her eyes off it. I mean, she *knows* I've only been married for six weeks. This is so embarrassing it's almost funny.'

'What are you talking about? What word?'

'Tryst!' Sara's voice catches on the final *t*, breaks into a laugh.

'Oh, *that* word.' Dave glances around, imagining himself, visibly, stripped of his rightful innocence. Sara shouldn't include him in this. One of the men has turned and is staring at them. He waits for Sara to look at him then tubes his lips and suctions in a lungful of air.

'Okay, buddy,' Dave says, 'you wanna keep those eyes in your head?' He imagines this to be a proper, endemic comment, one he would never make at home where a stranger, equally, would not be so obvious. Luckily, at the moment he considers the man's probable response – these people carry guns – there's a break in the traffic, and the group of men moves into the street.

Dave's knees weaken, in a familiar delayed response. In

Amsterdam, needing cigarettes, he wandered across short bridges over canals, unable to find a tobacconist. Seeing a vending box of the right size and shape mounted on a building wall, he stepped past several oddly-dressed women, pulling loose change from his pockets as he approached. The machine contained cello-boxed women's panties, scant wisps of devil red, midnight black. One of the women pointed at him, then bent her arm and thrust her fingers up her skirt. Harsh jeers broke the air. Dave checked himself, pacing his escape. His fingers closed over a mass of silver coins.

He went to Rome. To run away or to start over, he wasn't sure, although motion is not a complex form of energy, merely an obvious one. Several years later, he met Sara at a summer seminar in Cambridge. They kept in touch after that, exchanging letters, long distance calls, occasionally, as today, being in the same place at the same time; in Ottawa, once, in Banff, in San Francisco. Sara announced her engagement over chowder at Pier 31. 'I'm going to get married sooner or later,' she said. 'It might as well be now.' She was staying with friends in the Haight, and didn't have time to join him on the day's last ferry around Alcatraz. Dave went alone, separated by choppy water from an island where men lived their lives of isolation, dreamed their dreams of escape. He tried to call up a suitable emotion, sympathy or horror, but he didn't feel much of anything at all. The ferry returned and docked. His room, in a Traveller's Lodge, was walking distance from the wharf. A mime followed him part of the way, an exaggerated shadow in his peripheral vision. Dave resisted the urge to throw down a handful of bills, wait for the man to stoop to collect them, then kick him to death.

'THE PLACE we want is about twenty blocks north of here,' Sara tells Dave. The taxi has dropped them at an annex to the Whitney, and the annex is closed for renovations. He starts walking, not wanting to appear indecisive on the street. 'Are you going to be able to do it?' she asks. 'In those boots?'

'I wore them on purpose. I'm already numb from the knees

down, I can walk forever.' But he wishes he wasn't wearing a jacket. The sun has come out and evaporated the traces of rain on the sidewalk, lifting it into a thick, humid wall. By the time they reach 75th, he's wondering how it's possible to sweat so much and still have a full bladder. The gallery attendant won't let him use the washroom until he pays the four-dollar admission.

'It was worth every cent,' he tells Sara, when they're in the elevator, rising to the third floor and the Cindy Sherman exhibit. 'I would have paid, oh, ten or twenty dollars.'

'I should have warned you before we left. This city isn't real big on public facilities. Who knows, but they might be a toe-hold for Godless communism?' The elevator doors slide open, and Dave follows her down a short dog-leg of hall.

'I thought that was the ERA?'

'That too.' Sara grins, bumps her hip against his thigh. 'Don't you love this, being sophisticated?'

'Is that what we are?' Dave says, but he was thinking exactly that: he was thinking how far he's come from his first dinner in Tel Aviv, that attempt at worldliness. In the coffee shop at the Sheraton, he hastened to inform the waitress, 'I read up on the culture here before leaving home. You don't have to worry about *me* wanting bacon on my cheeseburger.' Taking her silence as a cue to continue, he suggested, 'I'm not sure if I'm legal to drink here, though. Maybe a vanilla milk shake?' After a long moment, the waitress asked him if he was from South Africa. 'Me? No, no. Not at all. Is that what I sound like?'

'Jesus, God,' he says, stopping at the entrance to one room. The pictures are about six feet high, three feet wide. Cindy Sherman spent ten years photographing herself in the poses, arranging her hair and make-up, her costumes. Dave read that much in *Esquire*, saw two pictures reproduced in the magazine, but he wasn't prepared for anything so vivid. There's a luminous quality to them, as though they were lit from behind. The colours are more real than the colours in real life.

Sara walks ahead of him, making small sounds of recognition

and appreciation, 'Uh-huh. Uh-huh, uh-huh.' Dave doesn't know what to do with his eyes. Cindy Sherman stares out from a curtained window, her nose red from crying; Sherman on a dock, looking back over her shoulder, terrified; Sherman dashed against a pebbled surface, her teeth and gums limned with blood. He follows Sara, hoping she isn't *identifying:* the images are violent, suffused with the horror of dailiness, the routine explosiveness worn one micron below the surface of everyday life.

He says, 'This isn't what I expected at all. None of this is predictable.' His voice sounds insincere, removed, but Sara matches his tone when she says, 'It's a really interesting way to use the familiar,' reassuring him he's on-key with a dispassionate, objective note. He's not to take this personally. He looks for line and balance and light source, the technique rather than content, so he can have an opinion rather than a reaction. Sara moves away when he's stopped in front of Sherman with a pig snout over her nose.

In the last room, a woman is sitting with a small child an a viewing couch, their backs to Dave. She is saying, in the overly bright, overly patient manner of someone whose resumé includes *Parenting,* 'The lady dresses up, just like you dressed up for Hallowe'en.' Dave controls his expression, circling around them, and gives her a middle-distance smile, a bland acknowledgement that, sometimes, strangers have to share space. Only after he turns to a wall of smaller, black-and-white photos, the neutral mattings a field for retinal after-image, does he realize the woman was breast-feeding an infant. He bends and squints at the pictures, trying to cut off his peripheral vision. He thinks, *Lady?*

At first, he considers the pictures to be stagy and meaningless: a woman on the sidewalk outside a small grocery; trapped on a median between two lanes of traffic: they look like establishing shots in old movies. He steps back, searching for a narrative, from left to right, and when Sara comes up beside him, he says, almost smug at having figured this out, 'All these women are three minutes away from being raped.'

'You should look over here.' Sara turns him towards the far wall. 'It's the same women four minutes later.'

'I DON'T KNOW what it'll be like when I start teaching next week,' Sara says. 'But it's nice now. We have breakfast together, then Martin goes off to work and I watch Donahue. Then I read, or futz around the house, until it's time to do a little dinner thing.'

'Six weeks,' Dave says, nodding. 'So you're still boning chicken breasts and cooking with wine.'

'Yes, as a matter of fact.' Sara looks down at her hands. 'What, you don't think it'll last?'

'I don't know what your course load is like, but I'd say, oh, maybe by January, you'll be pitching Lean Cuisines into the microwave.'

'When did you get cynical?'

'Me? I'm not. I might be a little more realistic, is all.' They've stopped at Bryant Park. Dave stretches his legs in front of him. There's a wide sidewalk, then a thick ground cover of ivy around a drained and dry fountain, its interior weathering towards the state of the Parthenon. Past that, a woman is sleeping on a bench in mirror-image to where he's sitting. Dave's jacket is dropped over his lap, and he has to lift it by the collar to take his cigarettes from the inside pocket.

'Even being here,' he says, exhaling a thin stream of smoke, the first, utilitarian drag. 'I'm not here for any of the reasons I planned.'

'And what were they?'

'Let's see, I was in, I think, grade five. I'm not sure what I was doing home from school, but I watched an afternoon movie called *Hatful of Rain*. It's about this guy who comes back from the Korean, uh, police action, with a tidy heroin habit. His wife has been working in a truly horrible typing pool and saving his pay so he can open a garage with his brother and father, I think. One day she passes out at her desk, because she's pregnant and, of course, she has to be fired. Meanwhile, the guy's telling his father he's run though his life savings because he's a junkie, and the father says something like, "So, stop being one."

'I don't remember the fifties, but they must have been really easy to live through. Unless they were impossible.

'Anyway, there's a scene where he's run out of credit with his dealer, and it's the archetype of every sleazy, desperate deal ever televised. The dealer makes the guy call him "Mother."

'My hair stood on end, and my eyes were like this,' Dave raises his hands to circle his fingers in a raccoon mask. 'At the end the guy's wife, Eva Marie Saint, no less, throws a blanket over him while he's going through withdrawal and ... she phones the police.' Dave drops his cigarette and twists it out with the toe of his boot. 'I was stretched out in front of the television, in my jammies and wrapped in a quilt, and I thought, "Jesus, *God*, when I grow up I'm going to live in Manhattan and be a heroin addict."' Beside him, Sara bursts into a gratifying laughter. Dave fists one hand in front of his mouth and says, 'I thought you'd like that. I do have a history of sort of missing the point.'

'But what happened?' she asks. 'Why'd you change your mind?'

'Oh, you know. Things.' Dave looks down. The summer of his first year of college he'd flown from a motorcycle, set skyward by a ton-weight of spinning Corvair. Grounded like Icarus, he'd lain in a hospital bed with his crushed legs sewn together, the skin from one stretched and stitched over the other so his life wouldn't leak out from either. His heart's scars may not be visible to the naked eye, but his calves, undressed, resemble slub-knit Argyle socks. The rest of his college years are blurred. His regular family doctor had taken a look at the surgeon's legacy and pulled a prescription pad closer to his writing hand. 'I think it was about a year later I saw Jefferson Airplane on Ed Sullivan, and decided it wasn't the Manhattan part I was looking for. Or maybe I got distracted.'

'Grace Slick was on *Donahue*,' Sara says. 'With a panel of recovering alcoholics. She's been dry for a year or two.'

'I wish you hadn't told me that. I'd like to believe there were some constants in life.' Dave takes out his last cigarette, holds it in his mouth and tosses the empty package towards a wire trashbin on his left. He misses, and gets up to do his part to keep the city clean. A large man in a not-so-large jogging outfit reaches the bench, stops behind him. Dave drops the package into the bin, turns back. The man moves away and Sara cups one hand, motioning to Dave. Just then, he sees that ivy behind the bench is rustling, not from the wind because there is no wind – he can't believe this – the ground cover is swarming with mice.

'Look, look,' he says, pointing. The cigarette drops from his mouth, but he leaves it on the sidewalk, hardly noticing. He's close enough to see the tiny shell-shapes of the mice's ears, but they won't be real unless she verifies their existence.

'Christ!' Sara leaps from the bench and turns to face the ivy. 'They're not rats, are they?' She bends forward, from the waist, not too close. 'They're like white mice,' she says then, calmly. 'But they're brown.'

Dave stands beside her, watching. He can't name his emotion, but it feels like the response to a sunset, or a dessert with whole raspberries, or seeing three women in pink hats in the back seat of a Blue Line cab.

There's a noise behind them, and they turn together. The woman has awakened from the park bench and is having a loud argument with the air in front of her. Her face reddens, she swings her arms wildly. A flash of white shows through a tear in her dark sweater.

'Dear, dear,' Sara says sadly. 'I was hoping she was normal.'

'The woman was sleeping with her head on a paper bag full of doorknobs,' Dave starts, but he changes his mind before finishing the sentence. 'She probably is,' he says. 'She couldn't have known how it was going to turn out when she signed up for the whole seventy years. We really take our chances.'

'There are some compensations,' Sara says. 'Can we go? I don't want to be here any more.'

They start walking. Dave's pleased that Sara has no plans for dinner on her own. She suggests an Italian place, not far from Penn Station, and they decide to have a drink in his room.

'I shouldn't eat too early,' she says. 'Or I'll end up going someplace else, after, and I don't want to be hanging the last dog. I'm getting an early bus tomorrow.'

'Okay, not a late night,' Dave agrees. 'I'm glad you told me about the Sherman thing, and were here today,' he adds. Delayed thank-yous too often sound like goodbyes. 'I might have been overwhelmed on my own. You know, all the dangers of the big city.'

'It can be intimidating,' she says vaguely. 'That's an interesting title, *Hatful of Rain*. What did it mean?'

'Don't ask me,' Dave shrugs. 'I was ten years old, not exactly an age for subtlety.'

WHEN DAVE drapes his jacket over the back of the desk chair, he notices the colour has rubbed off his shirt onto the lining. He lifts his shirt away from his chest, flapping the fabric, and ducks to check himself in the mirror. Sara sits on the small couch on the other side of the room. The bed is between them, as tidily made as a biscuit.

'I'll get ice.' Dave carries the plastic container into the hall, hearing, too late, the door click shut behind him. His key-card is in a jacket pocket; he'd taken it from his wallet during the elevator ride up. When he returns with the bucket filled, he has to knock. Sara calls out, 'Who is it?' and he rejects his name, or 'Room service,' or 'Vice squad,' in favour of a simple, 'It's me.'

Dave washes his hands before he touches the ice. The fine soap from his basket of complimentary toiletries has been replaced with a standard hotel issue. Having two glasses, and only the cap of the scotch to use as a jigger, he ends up moving back and forth from the bathroom to the desk three times.

'Surely there's a way to work this out in advance,' he says. 'Like those math problems, if seven people want to cross a river on a ferry which can only hold three at a time, what's the least number of trips necessary?' He carries a drink to Sara, then sits on the end of the bed with his own.

'I always liked those puzzles.' She holds up her glass, 'What do you say in Canada, that Eskimo thing?'

'*Gretzky.*' Dave raises his glass. 'To all the Wabasso sheet salesmen drinking in hotel rooms the world over.' He takes a mouthful. The ice hasn't much cooled the liquid.

'You *have* got cynical,' Sara laughs. She looks into her glass. 'It's good,' she says. Then, 'Are they alone, those salesmen?'

'Always,' Dave nods. 'Even when they're with women worth three and four hundred dollars.'

There's a silence broken only by the thin whine of the air conditioner before Sara says, 'Worth is a subjective term.'

'It is, yes,' Dave agrees. He finishes his drink and stands. 'How many trips do I have to make for a refill?'

'One, return. Put the scotch in, here, then carry the top to the tap with you.'

'That'll work. You are good at those.'

'I wouldn't have liked them if I wasn't.' She holds out her glass. 'You could double the result without twice the energy, if you get me another now.'

Dave shakes his head, impressed. 'No wonder you're the professor,' he says.

WHEN THE AIR greys to dusk in the room, Dave snaps on the floor lamp, which creates only a yellow pool like a urine stain over the carpet. He leaves his empty glass on the desk and returns to sit on the end of the bed, where the spread dips into a nest from his weight.

'Twilight is God's way of announcing dinner time,' he says. 'Do you think I have to dress?'

'Not if it'll show me up. I don't have anything to change into.'

'Maybe my boots.' Dave raises one foot, cups the heel in his hand and pulls. The move is unsuccessful. He stretches both feet in front of him, hooking the heel of one boot into the instep of the other. The effort makes him grunt and lean back on the bed, anchoring himself on his elbows.

'Do you need some help?' Sara asks, standing.

'No, no. I can do it. I've only had to sleep in them twice.' He feels his heel slipping against leather, and he starts to kick, to free his foot. The boot drums against the floor, then slips off. 'One down.' Dave stands, tipped to the side, and tries scraping the second boot against his socked foot. There's no friction, no grip. He drops back on the bed. 'I could wear one boot and one shoe,' he says, 'as long as I don't have to do any running.'

'Like in the park.'

'What?' Dave looks up at Sara. 'I didn't run.'

'No, not you. But I wanted to. There was that man, when you were looking at the mice? He showed me what he had in his jogging pants.'

'What did – oh. Oh!' Dave presses his hands into the mattress, sitting up straight. His feet are touching the floor, raising his knees to uneven heights. He can't think of anything to say. He covers the toe of his boot with his other foot, polishes it with his sock.

'You're never going to do that by yourself. Let me.'

Sara steps in front of him, bends her knees as if she's going to kneel down. Dave's hand, a stranger to him, shoots out and strikes her shoulder.

'It's *okay,*' he says, but his voice is drowned when she falls back against the wall and bursts into tears. He looks at his hand, still suspended in the air, a mottled yellow and pink paw. He folds three fingers against his palm, like a boy creating a gun for the games requiring someone be mortally wounded. Turning his wrist, he brings the pointing finger, the barrel, close to his temple. He levers his thumb up, cocking the hammer. At the moment when he should bear down with the folded fingers, squeezing the trigger, his hand drops to the bed, missing his lap. He doesn't feel it against his thigh. The shape of his body is a poorly defined constellation around the heart beating its two syllables: *My life,* it says, or *Courage.*

Signals

BRIAN'S MOTHER has started watching a lot of television, mostly cops-and-robbers dramas on one of the cable stations, and she's become very specific in her apprehension of a criminal network in the suburb where she lives.

'There was a '78 Dodge van parked across the street all of yesterday afternoon. In front of the old Pinney place? They might be casing the joint.'

Brian takes a deep drag from his cigarette, to keep from laughing into the phone. The tone she has adopted, in character with her cynical, vigilante role, is amusing enough to stop him from questioning her belief that evil is external, identifiably *they*. Some residual Catholic confusion surfaces briefly: Is his mother's belief heretical? Is his own? He lets this pass unexamined. And politeness alone stops him from questioning her belief that since he's home at eight-thirty on a Wednesday evening his time is available to her.

Across the room, Beaver mouths, 'Your mother?' and holds up the bottle of scotch. Brian nods, affecting a heavy world-weariness, and raises four fingers pressed together to indicate the size of drink he needs. As Beaver passes, on his way to the kitchen for ice, he runs one hand up the inseam of Brian's jeans, and makes loud kissing noises into the air. Brian covers the mouthpiece with his cigarette hand, making a threatening grimace. But then he pats at Beaver's ass, tight in his own jeans. Mixed signals.

'That's what they do, you know. They learn your hours. They could know when I'm not here and just load up that van with everything I own. The neighbours wouldn't notice a thing.'

'Your neighbours? They would so. They'd be over in a flash to make sure those burglars had clean clothes and recent haircuts.' This is why Brian isn't too worried about his mother being alone in the big house where he grew up. The street is still, despite his mother's suspicions, an old-fashioned neighbourhood, with women who watch out windows recording events, daytimes, to share with each other over the phone, evenings. Brian still smarts a bit at this network, although it's been sixteen years since it conveyed to his parents the news that Brian, at fourteen, had been spotted downtown, smoking. This intelligence made it home before Brian himself and imagining the neighbours' involvement – their culpability – made him feel doubly punished, victimized.

Growing up, Brian hated anyone to have power over him. He despised even how his sister Carole, eighteen months older, could make his life miserable in petty, absolute ways – 'I'll tell mom. Mom!' – and he dreamt of being an only child. Now Carole is living in Vermont with a not-divorced man (which may or may not have killed their father, depending on their mother's magnanimity when she brings this up) and Brian feels the weight of being his mother's only accessible child. She needs him, and Brian resents being obligated. He sees his childhood as something like a compulsory cocktail party. Now that a decent interval has passed, his attendance has been noted, it's time to find the hostess, shake hands and say goodbye, perhaps arranging a lunch date for some time in the middle future.

He takes another drag of his cigarette and realizes he's exhaling carefully, away from the receiver, so his mother won't hear him. When Beaver hands him drink, he takes a deep pull, miming excessive need for Beaver's benefit. Beaver only shrugs and moves over to start a deliberately casual inspection of the bookshelves. Beaver's real name is Michael Hinther, a secret almost as well kept as his real age, which is twenty-six. Brian knows this because he found Beaver's driving licence when he was looking through his wallet for a laundry ticket. But if Beaver wants to be, forever, nineteen, that's fine with Brian. People should be able to create themselves as best they can, to his mind; any other reality is just another version of original sin. The trick of it is, of course, that the self-creation has to be absolutely seamless.

He thinks his mother would worry less if she got out of the

house more. She's still an active woman, or could be, sixty-something isn't old any more, and he considers square-dancing groups, bus tours to historic sites, elaborate picnics with huge smoked hams, whole roast chickens. And white linen tablecloths, that's a nice touch. He doesn't suggest these things to his mother; she has a perverse streak that might surface. He can imagine her, spitefully, instead joining a singles brunch group, tinting her hair to a colour like Apricot or Champagne, and becoming one of those brittle, preserved women with their talk of eye-lifts, isometrics, diets, and men with American Express Gold Cards. Brian sees these women at some of the places he goes to – places with names like Dinkies and Little Eden and Wallbanger City – and suffers for their exposure of tooth and nail, their trying to hold on. He thinks his mind is not large enough to contain the concept of 'mother' in tandem with 'bikini waxing'.

'The silver would get top price from a fence these days.' There is something casually satisfied in his mother's voice, as if the theft has already occurred and, with much grace, she is not saying, 'I told you so.'

'No, no, I took that to the bank.' Brian sits up, alarmed. Beaver turns from the bookshelves, a large paperback of David Hockney prints open in his hands. 'You didn't bring that back to the house, did you?'

'Not the good silver,' she says quickly. 'The second best.'

'Oh, the plate.' Brian sits back, relieved. Since turning thirty, he's developed a sense of personal responsibility to the concept of history, a desire, perhaps, to have his place and time in the world marked, accounted for. Although he finds no room in his own life for clutter and ritual – his future is not clear enough to him for the commitment that would suggest: What does he want to be when he grows up? – he feels this is possible because his past is kept elsewhere, all in a piece. He can always start over.

'On Saturday, when you're here,' his mother goes on.

'I'm coming Saturday?'

'For dinner. And I want you look over this brochure I got from the cable company. They have some kind of alarm system for the house. I can't make out how it works. Do you suppose it hooks up to the television?'

'I'll have a look at it.

'My mother,' he announces to Beaver, unnecessarily, after hanging up.

'I thought we were going out Saturday.'

'We never go out before ten. I can do both.'

'You mean, you can fit me in?'

'Getting a little close in here, isn't it?' Brian carries his drink across the room. From the window he can see all the way down Century Street, right to the centre of town. On some still nights in the early spring and fall, if he has the windows open and the stereo off, he can hear the bells of the City Hall clock. He doesn't open the window in the summer – from June to September he rents an air conditioner – because nine floors below, along one side of the parking lot, are all the garbage bins from his building and the Cantonese restaurant next door. In July, however, he can see the fireworks exploding silently in the black sky framed by the window, more real than they would be if he was out in the evening, distracted by the sounds of children up past their bedtimes, solicitous parents, hawkers and vendors, even the crackle and boom of the fireworks themselves. This makes up for not hearing the bells in the summer, when they might make him nostalgic for the sounds he used to hear carried over the lake at his parents' summer place. He would lie in his dark room, listening, and wonder how many hours had passed since he was sent to bed, how many hours until morning. It's been a while since his assumption was, naturally, that tomorrow would be a day better than today.

Brian turns the knob to Low Cool and opens the exhaust. The created breeze sends six or seven dust bunnies scurrying across the bare floor, to hide under the couch.

'Did I ever tell you how tidy I am?' Beaver asks. 'I even do windows. A rare thing, let me tell you.'

'Don't start,' Brian warns. He recently read an editorial that suggested the phrase 'postal service' was oxymoronic. He laughed and tried to think of his own. The only thing that came to mind was 'healthy relationship.'

'Or you'll make me leave before the piggies?' Beaver asks, grinning. But he adds, 'Do you want me here or not?' with the inflection of a real, not rhetorical question.

What Brian wants is not to have the choice. When he started high school he was given a list of elective subjects and told to fit two into his timetable. The Typing he wrestled with as though it were a difficult, foreign language. 'J' he would translate, 'right hand, first finger, home row.' Only by staying after school, the tock-tock of the old Underwood hollow and forlorn in the empty room, was he able to pass the course, with a dismal eleven-words-a-minute in a class that averaged thirty-four. The Latin, actually being a foreign language, went somewhat better, although it remains isolated in his mind, a singular pocket of clauses and cases too explicit to apply to anything else. Since, he has been suspicious of that gift – choice – and looks for the deprivation in abundance, the catch.

'*Exigent sum,*' he says. He puts his drink down on the willow blanket hamper he uses as a coffee table and stretches his hands in front of him, fingers laced, knuckles cracking. 'Old bones. Can we talk about something else?'

'Of course,' Beaver says, disingenuous. 'So.' He sits on the arm of the couch, his feet hooked around the leg so he can lean back with his spine straight, six inches clear of the cushions. 'How is your mother?'

'She thinks someone is watching her house.'

'Really, where does she live?'

'I never told you?' Brian names the suburb, shaking his head. 'I can't think of a safer place. Practically her whole life is there. My whole life is there.'

'I can understand that,' Beaver says, sitting up properly and crossing his legs, ankle over knee. One of his socks has snared a dust bunny and his foot looks haloed, diffuse. 'It would be easy enough to think of time past as something taken away, and want to hold on to other things. Aging as a kind of violation. I do not have that kind of trauma, myself, you understand. Not yet. I'll save that one for my own sunset years.' He tilts his head to one side, framing his face with his hands, palms out. 'I'll think about it tomorrow,' he says.

'Beaver,' Brian says. 'That's very near profound, what you said.'

'I am only shallow,' Beaver says, with great dignity, 'on the surface. I know as much about insecurity as the next guy. It's about losing control.'

From the open book on the coffee table, Hockney's portrait of his own parents faces up. Brian slumps back, against the window frame. Is there a Latin word for *window?* Beaver gets up and stands close beside him. He smells warm and cottony, like fresh ironing. Brian puts his arm around him, across the small of his back, and holds him, idly considering what anyone who looked up through the window would see. Both men are roughly the same height, over five ten but under six feet, with the medium-dark colouring Beaver calls 'low Episcopal'. Brian hopes their attraction suggests, for each of them, a healthy self-image.

He lightly rests his chin on Beaver's shoulder, looking down. Mrs. Hockney sits in a plain trestle-chair, her hands clasped in her lap, staring intently forward. Off to her left, Mr. Hockney is in profile, bent from the waist to examine closely a large book held open in his lap. Mr. and Mrs. Hockney.

'So, you want me to stay?' Beaver asks in a quiet voice. 'Or do we just have this warm moment?'

'Tonight,' Brian says. 'I want you to stay tonight.'

BRIAN TEACHES high school science. Tries to teach, rather; the marking is not going well. 'What is the coloured part of the eye?' he asked on the exam. 'Cones,' fully one-third of the class responded. A bonus question, 'How many eyes does a bat have?' had been read as a trick, and most of the students answered, 'None.'

What is going on here? he wonders. When he was their age he

was experimenting with drugs, but he doesn't see any signs of that in his classes. The kids' eyes are clear and untroubled, evidently only their minds are unfocused. How is he supposed to reach them, to make them thrill to verifiable principles? He wants to shake them up, to yell, 'You little bastards, this kind of inattention is just selfishness!' But his chance has passed, he is supposed to hand in the low-pass grades and wait until September for another.

He pushes the unmarked papers into a file folder, checks to make sure he has his wallet and keys, glances at his watch. He's due at his mother's at five, then to meet Beaver at Little Eden at ten. It's two-thirty.

The hardware store is in an underground mall below a chain hotel. Brian parks on a metered side street and enters the hotel lobby, where there is a bank of elevators. A man is waiting there, and he nods as Brian stands beside him, hands held behind his back. 'Hello.' The man's voice is deep, with a slight rhythmic inflection. A Norwegian accent, something like that. He has the pale looks of the actor who played Jackal in that movie. Brian thought he was attractive, although Beaver's opinion was that the actor's teeth looked like a snow fence in March.

'Hello,' Brian says. The elevator arrives and Brian steps back to let the man enter first. He presses 12; Brian, M-1. There is a long delay after the doors slide closed. Brian pushes the button marked Close Door, to encourage the mechanism. He looks at the other man and makes a faintly apologetic shrug. He doesn't want to appear impatient, but he doesn't want to be defeated by a machine, either.

'Are you in the hotel?'

'No, I live in town,' Brian says, then looks at the elevator panel, the conflicting instructions: up and down. 'I wasn't thinking.'

The man appears to give this careful consideration. He nods. The elevator shudders and starts up.

'I am the winner, then.'

'I guess you are,' Brian agrees.

On the twelfth floor the man steps out, then turns back. 'Coming?' he asks, and Brian steps out of the elevator. Following him down the hall, Brian watches the centre seam of the man's jacket, where the pattern meets in a solid colour like the no-passing line on a highway. He hears the elevator slide closed and the car, unoccupied, moving down.

The hotel room has a double bed, an upholstered chair, a combination desk and dresser, colour television bolted to a wall shelf, and a rollaway cot, open and made.

'What's this?' Brian asks, pointing. 'Are you expecting someone?'

'Don't talk, please,' the man says, shrugging out of his jacket. 'Say nothing.'

Brian, silent, raises his hand to unbutton his shirt cuff. This is, after all, the other man's fantasy.

SYPHILIS, he thinks. Gonorrhea. Jesus, herpes. But panic stays back, guilt refuses to land. His afternoon was a minor corruption, no worse, really, than the parking ticket he has stuffed into the glove compartment. Already, this is in the past, a closed chapter. He swings wide, turning. The car's muffler scrapes on the slope of the driveway, and the rough sound brings Brian's mother to the front door. She calls out as he slides the shift into Park. He can't make out her words, her voice competing with a lawnmower somewhere in the neighbourhood. He lets himself out of the car and stands in the wedge between the open door and the car's body.

'Right on time,' she says, stepping quickly along the sidewalk. She is wearing a skirt and blouse, flat-heeled shoes and looks, Brian thinks, to be about forty. Where, in the face of this evidence, does he get his ideas of what ages look like? Maybe from Beaver. He can imagine, while he's sleeping, a slow osmosis of values, the pores of his skin open and receptive. His mother makes quick, patting touches on his forearm. They're not the type to hug. 'You look all bright-eyed and healthy,' she says. 'Have you been jogging?'

'You know me better than that,' Brian says. 'I guess it's just clean living.'

'Even as a child you were healthy. Both my children were, although your sister had that awful skin in her teens. Remember? Pizza-on-toast you called it.'

'A sensitive child,' Brian mumbles.

'I wonder if that man knows what she looked like? He must have seen photographs, surely. Maybe I should send some, for Christmas.'

'Meow,' Brian says. 'Sensitivity must run in the family.' He waves across the street and is rewarded by a twitching of Mrs. Chiccini's drapes. 'You're being watched,' he tells his mother, and she shakes her head, clucking. Brian slides one of the cardboard boxes from the back seat of the car and lays it at her feet. 'I stopped at the hardware store and got you these.'

She bends and pulls one of the screens from the box. As she holds it up to the sky, her face is dappled with the light that passes through the grill, shapes like the clubs in a deck of cards.

'It's very heavy,' she says. 'Pretty, though. What's it for?'

'They're for the basement windows,' Brian says, lifting the other box from the back seat. 'I'll show you.'

IN THE BASEMENT, as he works, Brian develops an easy, competent rhythm: screws sink themselves in flush security; crumbling mouldings form themselves into right angles under his hands; he feels masculine and charismatic. Above him, the house has the not-unpleasant weight of an adult decision. After he's done four of the six windows, his mother appears at his elbow, surprising him. He'd forgotten she lives here.

'You look so intense,' she says. 'Men at work.'

Brian wipes his hand across his forehead. The gesture is for his mother; even in summer the basement is cool, and the work is not difficult. 'I'd like to finish today.'

'I could bring your dinner down here,' she says. 'We could set up the card table, like a little picnic indoors. It's chicken.'

Brian remembers the card table. One winter when school was

closed by an outbreak of strep throat he and Carole, spared, had played endless games of Go Fish. 'Mom!' he remembers his sister's voice. 'Mom, Brian says he doesn't have any eights and I saw one in his hand.' 'Why are you looking at your brother's cards?' asked from the top of the stairs. 'I am trying,' Carole said, smug and wise, 'to keep him honest.'

'Come here, I want to show you how these work.' He slides one of the windows open. He's installed the metal screens between the two panes of glass. 'You see, you can still open them, for air, but nothing else. And you can't remove them from outside, only from down here.'

'I see,' his mother nods. 'Aren't you clever? Your father was never good with his hands. Not that I minded, but it seems a man should be able to do things around the house, not call a repairman for every fuse and fan belt.' She shakes her head. 'The money that goes on repair, just maintenance things, ordinary wear and tear. It's history now, but when I think of the days I sat around waiting for the plumber or the furnace man.' She makes a tetch-sound with her front teeth.

'A house is a big responsibility,' Brian agrees. 'But it has its rewards, your own place.'

She slides the window closed, then back open, and doesn't comment. 'What about if there's a fire?'

'Leave the building in an orderly fashion.' It's what Beaver would say, an automatic response no longer requiring thought. 'I don't know,' he admits. 'I didn't think about getting out. Maybe you just better not start any fires down here.'

'I'm sorry. I didn't mean to slight your work. But my concern isn't only for real estate.'

'Weren't you going to get me some dinner?' Brian asks.

'Oh,' his mother says, slipping into the tone of voice most familiar to Brian. 'You never liked any kind of disagreement.'

'That's right.' Brian turns away from her, back to work.

WHEN SHE BRINGS down the tray of fried chicken, green and yellow wax beans, roast potatoes, Brian is surprised to see an opened bottle of beer, half-poured with a neat head into one of the cut-glass water tumblers. The only times he drinks at his mother's are when he brings wine for dinner, at Thanksgiving and Christmas.

'Did you get this for me?'

She looks flustered, and smooths her hands over her skirt several times, her eyes glancing from the furnace to the stationary tubs, avoiding Brian.

'What?' Brian grins, unable to imagine what's caused this reaction. 'Did I say something?'

'It's not that.' She looks at him levelly, with some effort. 'I got the beer for Mr. Daly.' There is a proud note in her voice, an enviable possessiveness.

'Daly? From one-forty-three?' Brian steps over to the window, tip-toes up to look in the direction of that house number. 'Him?'

'I just happened to mention that the washer was giving me some trouble. The spin cycle? And he offered to look at it. Well, I didn't think I could offer him coffee or tea in the middle of the afternoon, a grown man.'

'No, I guess you couldn't.' Brian raises the glass and takes a sip of beer, toasting his new status. 'And the washing machine?' he asks.

'Oh, it's fine,' she says quickly. Then, 'You're teasing me.'

'Just a little,' Brian admits. But to keep the joke contained, before it can become a part of the family, he waggles a chicken leg at her with a cautioning gesture. 'There are some things a son doesn't have to know, okay?' She looks up at him, inhaling with a short gasp, and Brian steps back, suddenly serious. 'When I finish these windows,' he says. 'Do you understand? Once I finish these windows, nobody will be able to get in here. Nobody.'

TRYING TO KEEP a safe distance between himself and a black Trans-Am, Brian misses his turn and has to circle the block to get into the parking lot behind Little Eden. It's a few minutes past ten, but still he takes his time locking the steering column, rolling up the window, snapping off the radio so it won't crackle and blare when he starts the car later. He knows he has been told, in a loopy, oblique way, that his mother will be needing him less. Instead of feeling unburdened, as he should, he feels that he has been accused of something, the sense he has when the phone rings and rings, then stops just as he picks up the receiver. A connection has been missed.

Inside, Little Eden is over-cooled, pleasant for Brian, who has driven with the car window open and feels his skin filmed with dust and exhaust, although he knows he will be clammy in a few minutes. He stands still, adjusting to the patterned light from Tiffany lamps, the music pumping into the room, then spots Beaver sitting with a very pregnant woman in one of the banquettes. Weaselling through the crush of bodies radiating from the centre bar, he steels himself to meet one of Beaver's 'young ladies'. Women attach themselves to Beaver, oblivious to the personal distance he maintains, constructing their own myths about a gentleman 'not like the others'. His sympathy for these women and their expectations is diluted by the pain they cause Beaver, his wide-eyed bewilderment, 'What did she want?' Brian can only shrug; it isn't in him to explain Beaver's charm, to answer what it is that might have been wanted. It may be desire, rather than 'sensibility' that Beaver mocks when he lists, 'Ralph Lauren sweaters, a fridge full of Perrier, and all the latest Broadway show albums. Welcome to the not-quite-real world.' Brian, unable to voice *Not me?* settles for a Brando mumble, responding, 'The banal. The banal.'

'I'm a little late,' he says, sliding into the banquette beside Beaver.

'That's okay,' Beaver says. 'I ordered for you.'

'Jesus, Beaver.' Brian has just noticed the drink at his place, a half pineapple, scooped out and filled with a viscous yellow fluid. This is topped with not one but two paper parasols. He has to laugh. 'What is it?'

'No one knows. The bartender just invented it. Margot made a few suggestions.'

'Margot.' Brian nods to acknowledge the introduction. He takes a tentative sip and winces, his back teeth registering an instant protest. He waves to stop a passing waitress and orders another round for the table, substituting a scotch for the pineapple. 'Thanks for trying,' he says to Beaver.

'Are you finished with this?' the waitress asks, putting one hand on the pineapple.

'Yes, I'm the scotch,' Brian says.

'After this, scotch?' she asks, putting the paper parasols on the table in front of Brian. 'You get to keep these.'

'Well, thank you,' Brian says. Under the table, Beaver's thigh is warm against his own. Across the table, Margot is lining up her empty glasses for the waitress to clear away.

'Scotch, after your nice drink?' Beaver asks when the waitress is gone. 'Don't you know, never mix never worry?'

'I guess my mother never told me that one. Is that what you learned at your mother's knee?'

'At my mother's knee I learned only what a bony knee looks like,' Beaver says quickly. It's obviously something he's said before. Then he looks down into his drink. 'Actually, the only things I remember her specifically telling me were, Always iron silk in one direction and, Never sleep with your face on a handbag. I think she wanted a daughter.'

'Really?' Brian starts to laugh, but controls himself. It's possible Beaver has shared with him something important and revealing. He's never mentioned his own mother before; he usually presents himself as having been created, complete, at nineteen. 'Listen,' he says, keeping his voice light. 'In an era of erroneous zones and being your own best friend, those are probably not bad rules to live by.'

'They're so important, rules to live by,' Margot says. She pushes her hair back from her forehead and Brian, who knows a story introduction when he hears one, composes the muscles of his face to look pleasant, interested. 'I had wanted,' she says, 'to have a perfect driving record – no demerits – and absolute fidelity in my marriage.' She had managed both, she tells them, until the afternoon her brakes failed and she zipped through a red light into the back of a parked police cruiser. After that, she blazed a trail of promiscuity that ended with a messy divorce and a painful pelvic inflammation. Telling this to Brian and Beaver, her face takes on the swollen, pouched look of a woman about to cry, and Brian tactfully suggests she might not want to finish her Comfort Stinger. 'Oh, drinking can't hurt me,' she says. 'I even drank castor oil. Have you ever? It's like trying to swallow Vaseline, you practically have to chew it.' She looks down at her tummy, shaking her head sadly. 'I'm just going to be preggy forever.'

Alarmed, Brian leaves some bills on the table and hustles Beaver out of Little Eden and into the car.

'Hey, don't let the breeders get you down,' Beaver says, then stops talking while Brian gentles the accelerator, trying to get the engine to turn over.

'The only thing worse than a machine is a machine that doesn't work,' Brian grumbles. Then, as his effort is rewarded, 'Don't say "breeders".'

'Yes, sir,' Beaver says. 'I didn't know it bothered you.'

'Well, it does.' Brian speeds up, to catch a green light before it changes. It doesn't bother him, not really. 'And I'm starting to feel a little guilty about leaving like that. Maybe you could tell her I'm manic-depressive or something?'

'Honesty's the best policy?' Beaver slides closer to Brian. The car seat dips and creases with a moist, puckering sound. 'I've never seen her before in my life. She said we could share the table.'

'Is that true?' Brian glances over at Beaver, side-lit by the passing streetlights. 'And she told you something that personal?'

'Who else would she tell? You wouldn't want to try that on your friends. They might change their opinion of you. Why risk it?' Beaver shrugs, an arcing, helpless motion Brian can feel through the car's seat.

They are silent. Brian, who has never in his life considered confiding in a stranger, is remembering the Norwegian's sudden talkativeness, after. He had thought the story was necessary to the man's idea of intimacy, a belief that he was not casual, had more than the one dimension. Perhaps that was the point of the fantasy: the silent, non-judgemental audience. He sees his building up ahead, the blocks of light on the sheer brick side facing Century, and has a vision of one person behind each window, lips moving silently, comforted by the words themselves, as if they had no meaning, were incantations or prayers so explicit they could not be translated into experience.

'Look at them,' Beaver says, as the car's headlights sweep the parking lot. There are three teenaged boys leaning on the hood of a car. They are all wearing jeans and black T-shirts with large, glittering decals on the front – Black Sabbath, Led Zeppelin, Grateful Dead – groups Brian has known and forgotten.

'Yeah, I see them,' he says. He used to call this 'hanging out' but his students say 'hacking around.'

'Ten years ago I would have been one of them,' Beaver says. 'Now I'm afraid of them. Even the Beaver doesn't get to be nineteen forever.'

'Oh, Beaver.' This admission is so close to what Brian was thinking, was feeling, he doesn't turn the car to back into his space, but leaves the engine idling as he opens his door. He has his back to Beaver when he says, 'Take the car. Go back to your place and get what you need, then come back. Okay?'

'What?'

'Toothbrush. Clean underwear. I don't know.' Brian's shrug restates Beaver's earlier one: Why risk it?

'Why don't you come with me?' Beaver asks, but he's sliding across the seat, taking his place behind the wheel.

'I don't want to do any choosing,' Brian admits. 'You do that. I'll be up there.'

'What if I come back with a coffee table or a television or something?'

'Then we'll live with a coffee table,' Brian says. He swings the car door closed, and stands to one side. Beaver backs out of the lot, tooting the horn before he eases onto Century.

Alone in his apartment, Brian considers having a quick shower, or at least changing his clothes. He is uncertain what he would want this to mean. It could be penance, or an alibi. The apartment is small and warm and he moves to turn on the air conditioner.

He stands at the window, looking down to where his car should be. The parking lot is like a wide smile, with a tooth missing. Once, watching out this same window, he had seen a road crew repair a pothole beside a storm grating. When they were done, one of the three men had opened the grating and, using a rake to extend his reach, had pulled from the sewer a travel bag, similar in size and shape to those sold by airlines. This one, however, was a solid burgundy colour and even from nine stories up looked expensive. The other two workers had moved in, blocking Brian's view, as the first held the bag open for their inspection. Then the bag was tossed onto the back of the open truck, where Brian could see it as the workers drove away. It sat on a neat pile of two-by-fours, visible until the truck turned off Century.

Why does he think of that now? It's less than half a story; he never learned any more than he had seen. Brian presses his forehead to the window. The breeze from the air conditioner is cool on his neck. The vibration through the glass tickles his ear. He hates not knowing how things turn out, whether or not a story has a happy ending.

DAYV JAMES-FRENCH was born on Prince Edward Island and has lived in most Canadian provinces as well as spending time in the British Isles, Europe and the Middle East. After graduating from Carleton University, he studied writing at the University of Victoria. His first short story appeared in *The Antioch Review* in 1985 and he has since published widely in Canada, the U.S. and Australia; stories have been included in *Best Canadian Stories* and *The Macmillan Anthology*. He lives in Ottawa with a psychologist and a cat.